wayne hopkins

in the flesh

Books by Wayne Hopkins

Far From Paradise (Collection)

At The Dead of Night (Novel)

Dog Day Summer (Novel)

First edition. Paperback. 2024. Cover illustration by Seweryn Vvilczy Jasiński.

https://linktr.ee/vvilczy

Social media tag: @vvilczy

Edited by Nora Jacobs

Published by Farris Books.

ISBN: 979-8-9867176-6-1 (Paperback)

ISBN: 979-8-9867176-7-8 (Ebook)

I

Introduction. Kayla and 'Birdy'. Salma Hayek.

I'm going to kill myself tonight.

Or maybe tomorrow—I'm not sure. Let's just play it safe and say that I'm killing myself after I finish writing this. It could take a while.

And that's fine by me, I'm in no hurry. It's not like suicide is going anywhere. Like my dad used to say, "It'll still be here when we get back." He was usually referring to my GameCube, but I think it can apply to killing yourself, too. I've dwelled on it for months now and not because I was hesitant to end it, but because they make suicide nearly impossible in state mental hospitals. If it were completely up to me, I would've done myself in long ago. Probably before I was even sentenced.

Man, I really blew it by sparing myself. It could have been so easy, almost effortless. What the hell was I thinking? Right after leaving Debra's, I could've bought a gun, went home, fed my fish, then shot myself in the face. Actually, scratch that. I wouldn't have gone to Debra's that night. In hindsight, that was one of my biggest mistakes.

I clearly didn't know that then, though. At that point, I still believed that I could undo everything.

It's almost laughable now. Like, I really thought that I was onto something…but considering how it all ended, I guess I kind of was. Be that as it may, I still don't have a clue what really happened. That's the funny part, I suppose. Despite everything that has occurred between meeting Christie and now, I'm almost as confused as I was when it first began.

But let's not get things twisted here. That's not why I'm doing it. I don't care if I'm confused; to be honest with you, I wouldn't even technically call myself crazy. Though before you ask, that's not what everyone at Chilton's will tell you. They'll all tell you that I'm insane, but of course they would! The whole staff met me while being a patient at a psychiatric hospital, for God's sake. What else are they supposed to think?

Don't worry, I'll get to the actual story soon. Truthfully, that's the only reason I'm writing this. This way I can tell the story my way, the best I can, from front to back, without somebody dismissing it and questioning my sanity. Therefore, it's a story you're in for, but also my way of signing off. Just think of it as a *looonnggg* suicide letter with dialogue.

But I guess we better establish who *you* are before we get started.

As eager as I am to write this, I'm not too sure who it's for. This journal could very easily go unnoticed and untouched by everyone. What does Chilton's staff do with personal belongings if there is no suitable family left behind to collect them? Do they just toss their shit? Am I writing this just so it can be thrown away?

Well, I'm hoping that isn't the case. I hope someone finds it and reads this. That's precisely why I'm leaving it in such a conspicuous place; right in between my bedframe and mattress. After I've offed myself, they'll remove my body, clean my room, and eventually find it.

I have this strong feeling that Kayla and Birdy are going to be the ones who end up reading this first. They're my usual nurses, and I don't think it's far-fetched to think they'll be the ones assigned to cleaning my room. Hopefully, they'll end up snooping through my stuff, too.

And if that's the case, I want to say something directly to them.

So, Kayla?... Birdy?...

Eat shit and die.

Seriously, go fuck yourselves. You two scary, skanky bitches are essentially the reason I'm ending it so soon. I might've been content here if it weren't for you two. Both of you are among the worst women I've ever met, and that's saying something because I used to get around. I've met my fair share of awful women, and trust me, you guys take the cake. Or at least share it with Adriana, but we'll get to her later.

The point is that you both suck. Honestly, WHY COULDN'T YOU TWO JUST STAY THE HELL AWAY FROM ME! Can't either of you take a hint? You both make every day the worst day of my life. Kayla, with your constant groping and smirking, and

Birdy, with your comments and stupid fake name. Fucking despicable...

So, I took some time to calm down after writing that last part and now I feel bad. It's really not their fault they're so vile and perverted. They probably don't even remember coming on to me...More than likely because it's never happened.

To Kayla and 'Birdy' I'm nothing but a coke-snorting, crypt robbing, grandma murdering maniac. Why on earth would they ever flirt with me? Easy, they're not and I'm just insa-

Whoops! Almost admitted it there. Well, not *admitted*. That would imply what the court said is true, and it most certainly isn't. So, let me be clear, I'm not insane—I just need to die.

There's nothing they can do for me psychologically. My death is the only real way that I can be free of this, no amount of therapy or medication can dispel the things I see. No siree; when it comes to the staggering case of Brady Morgan, the state of Illinois should've just sent me to the chair.

But apparently, they couldn't do that out of "good faith." Whatever the hell that means. I suppose the way I behaved at my trial sealed the deal with my attorney (Public defender) pleading insanity. Who would've guessed that screaming and vomiting in court and then shielding my eyes from the judge and prosecutor would lead to an insanity plea? How much *Law and Order* was I supposed to watch to know that one? Nevertheless, they threw me in the looney bin and tossed the key almost immediately. There wasn't a single chance of my freedom, nor was there a chance of being transferred to an actual prison where there's hardly any women and I could kill myself in peace.

Although, before we actually begin, I want to get one more thing across.

Let's just say that they did free me, right? All of a sudden, I'm a free man again and let's say it's even off my record. I'd still kill myself, no question about it. I wouldn't seek out a job, I wouldn't take drugs (maybe) and I definitely wouldn't be chasing sex like so many free men do. Not with a woman anyway. I guess I could still get with a man if I wan- wait, what am I saying? I'm not gay? Hold on, why did I put a question mark after that? I'm really not gay! I've never even been attracted to men… but then again, I'm not attracted to women anymore either.

Which is precisely my point.

Here, let me emphasize that even more. If I was a free man, PUSSY would be the last thing on my mind. Even if a woman helped me escape the hospital in daring fashion, and all she wanted was a kiss for her efforts, I still wouldn't let her near me. Nothing would change. I'd rather put my dick in a beehive than be locked in a room with a woman.

Right hand to God (you can't see me but I'm writing this with my left) I would even turn away Salma Hayek. She could be wearing her *From Dusk Til Dawn* outfit and I still wouldn't care. Her, Clooney, and that large python can go to hell.

I'm sorry to linger on this, but I feel it's necessary. Here's another example.

Even if Beyonce had texted me an album of nude photos that she *personally* took for me, I'd be livid as well as scared. I'd quickly change my number; I might even call the cops.

Oh, still don't get it? Picture Margot Robbie lustfully presenting herself on a king-sized bed. Pretty awesome, right? WRONG. I'd tell her to fuck off to the other side of the equator in a heartbeat.

And just so there's not any confusion, I'm not, nor have I ever been, a misogynist. Frankly, before all of this, I flat-out adored women. I *loved* them in every sense of the word. At one point in my life, I even daydreamt about having daughters someday. For a long time, women were all I ever thought about…

But now that admiration and adoration is long gone. It doesn't matter who it is or what the circumstances are, women of any age and shape, scare the living shit out of me. And not in the way that a preteen boy is scared of them. They don't make me nervous; they strictly terrify and repulse me.

And I'll finally tell you why that is, okay? It's a bizarre story, and I still have my doubts, but maybe you can figure it out. Personally, I get closer every day to embracing it as a total unsolvable mystery. Maybe I know all there is to know about it and it's time to let go. I mean, realistically that's what I'm doing whether there's more to learn or not.

Anyway, the story only starts one way and with one person.

It all began on our first date and the first time I saw Christie in the flesh.

II

How we met. How it went. How it ended.

'In the flesh' was pretty much my catchphrase back in my hay-day, which, for the record, was no further back than half a year ago. I almost want to cringe writing it down now, though. Today, it's hard for me to believe I used the phrase so leisurely; it just sounds so douchey. The worst part about it was that it never proved itself effective or did wonders for me anyway. Yet whenever I met up with a girl online, I'd always say the line in some fashion. Something along the lines of 'even more beautiful in the flesh'—or hotter, cuter, sexier. It all depended on the girl and the context really.

But there isn't a chance that I didn't realize how stupid I sounded back then. No matter how regularly I used it, the words always sounded forced coming out of my mouth. Every one of those women had to know I was full of it after that corny ass line.

Though then again, I imagine it would sound ingenuine coming out of anyone's mouth. I mean, who actually talks like that besides English majors and Count Dracula?

I must've thought that it sounded as smooth as glass when I first heard it. I probably ripped it off a movie I saw; that sounds like something I'd do. Apparently, I thought that it would help me sound elegant. Although, given that I met those girls on Tinder, I don't think they were chasing elegancy. It definitely wasn't listed on my profile.

If I had to wager why women decided to meet up with me, I'd say it was simply because of my appearance and nothing else. Not to brag, but I have some nice features women typically dug. They'd go on about my blue eyes, and I also have a thick head of dark hair, which only enhanced my colorful gaze. I wouldn't call myself a stud or anything, but I do all right—or did, I mean.

Additionally, my bio stated that I was six-foot—I'm actually five-ten, but trust me, they never knew the difference. Plus, it's not as if those women were truthful or looking for something serious anyway. Or else they wouldn't be on Tinder. I never wanted children personally, but something about meeting the love of your life on a hook-up app doesn't register as a cute story to tell your kids. The show *How I met Your Mother* would've been gross if they just met on Tinder, if not just ended after the first season.

As far as I was concerned most women on those apps just wanted a good spank and to be sent on their way. And, I, for one, was all for it. Who am I to deprive a woman of casual sex in this day and age? I was all for the cause. I'm what you would call an activist. Or an opportunist depending on how you look at it.

However, I have recently considered a different outlook. After some reflecting in my solitude — the fuck else am I going to do? —I've realized that I could have been overlooking my 'date's' intentions and only focusing on my own. Maybe some of these women actually wanted to get to know me? I'm not sure, it's hard to say. What I do know is that I never really wanted to get to know them.

That wasn't the case with Christie.

I still used my 'in the flesh' line though, and to which, she blushed and smiled abashedly. Now that I think about it, she was clearly letting me off easy with her reaction. She was probably embarrassed *for* me. I should've just been grateful she didn't turn around and ditch me on the spot.

She let me off the hook more than once while we were together, so it makes senses if she let shit slide on our first date as well. Honestly, she was too forgiving for her own good. Not only was she willing to give anyone the benefit of a doubt, Christie was also modest despite the fact she was a fuckin' dime.

She had this think-about-what-you-say look to her that surely intimated a lot of men. It probably had something to do with her luscious but wild black hair and her pale green eyes. Christie had a good sense of style, too. At times she partly looked like she could be in a metal band or married to a criminal—or be a criminal herself.

Come to find out she was none of those things.

My bad, I'm getting a little ahead of myself. Before writing this, I told myself I wouldn't drag on, so I might be overlooking a few things. I meant to tell you about the first time I saw a picture of her.

Similar to more than half of the women I hooked up with in my twenties, I first saw Christie on the wonderful sticky world of Tinder. I was having a late night (per usual) when I received the notification. More specifically, I was slouched, lounging on the couch and brainlessly scrolling through my feed when she must've swiped right on my profile.

Now, I'm not sure if you've ever been on Tinder, but it's a cyber cesspool of bimbos, tools, losers, and the horny. All in all, everybody on the app is fairly desperate, and that included myself.

If you've never been on, it consists of swiping either left or right on Tinder profiles in your area; left being no, right being yes. But the only way you can actually match with someone is if you've both swiped right on each other's profile. With that being said, I swiped right on almost everyone. Doing so generally improved my chances of getting ass, if not just boosting my self-confidence from all the matches I'd get.

That tactic never failed me either. My phone would regularly light up with matches. Though, just because I matched with them didn't mean we would meet up every time. It simply made picking easier.

The majority of straight women on Tinder expect the man to send the first message. And I never really had any issue with that, because it allowed me to pick my 'battles'. Very rarely did a woman ever hassle me for a date or meet up. Like most men, I was the one inquiring.

I'd send the initial message and then that would lead to a brief period of small talk. Or, if they were the straight-forward type, it'd be cut-to-the-chase talk. Dealing with people on dating/hook-up apps is a toss-up. Some people want to build trust while others are as direct as a sex worker.

I don't exactly remember the very first time I saw Christie's profile. but I wasn't shocked that I swiped right on it. As noted, she was bangin'. Whenever I got familiar with her bio, my first impression was a hopeful one, but in a different way than it played out.

I first assumed that she was a kinky lay, which I *was* heavily into. As long as she didn't like water sports or poo-play, I was onboard…Unless she was down with furries, or liked cuckold activities. Nothing against the cucks out there, but if you're into that stuff, maybe keep your coaching down to a minimum. Last time I was cuckolding for a couple, the husband coached me like I was in there with Apollo Creed and he was Micky. "*You gotta get mean, Rock!*"

Anyhoo. I actually got around to reading Christie's bio once we matched. Below photos of her at a live show, in a sunflower meadow, and a few selfies, her bio read: "Wanna-be actress in the Windy City. I probably swiped right because I saw a dog in your profile. And no, I won't be your goth GF for Halloween. Quit asking."

Based off her bio, I should have known that she was going to be trouble. A fucking actress? She was bound to be a handful. And the fact that she was a *preforming* actress, like on stage, in a city like Chicago, just meant she had bigger balls than me. I could never do anything like that.

I didn't know what her intentions on Tinder were, but once we began to chat, I wasn't sure what mine were either. I know that sounds like a croc of shit, but Christie was that good looking. I wasn't fully committed to approaching it seriously (come to find out I never was) though I'd be lying if I said I didn't dwell over it a little.

She was the kind of woman a man sees and instantly wants to bag as his girlfriend.

And that went double for me after we met in person.

A one-night stand wasn't what she had in mind.

We decided to meet up at a hibachi spot in northern Chicago, and after my stupid line, we went on a to have the best first date I've ever been on. Despite all the terrible events that followed, it's still impossible for me to resent our first evening together.

On top of being stunning, Christie was also an all-out *riot*. She loved to laugh and all night she humored me with her edgy sarcasm and the observations she made. I was legitimately blown away from how hilarious she was. And it wasn't in the way women are typically funny around men; she wasn't ditsy or whimsy, Christie was SUPER inappropriate and halfway mean. I was absolutely smitten.

Throughout our date I kept finding things I found interesting about her. Almost everything about her had some depth to it. Before our first date I learned that her full name was Christie Marie D'Angelo, which is objectively a sexy name just looking at it. I loved hearing all about her aspirations with art, and her biggest dreams, and more importantly, she seemed to love sharing them with me.

Our silences were even peaceful at the start. During the downtime of our first date, I sat across from her and would watch her green pensive eyes survey the room. I remember desperately wanting to know what she was dwelling on. That was something I never did with anyone else. I never gave a damn what the person across from me was thinking. It didn't seem to matter until I met her.

Not going to lie, I was obsessed with how she made me feel. I've had steady girlfriends before, but Christie was already different. I loved how she kept me occupied and had a totally different spin on things than I did. I even began to think being around her was healthy; she wasn't as jaded as everybody else around me at that point.

After the date, I resisted bombarding her with sweet texts and even avoided fantasizing about her. I didn't want to get my hopes up... Again, I know it sounds corny, but I needed to know she felt remotely the same way. That night I was as lovestruck as a boy in junior high, I just didn't let her know that. Not until she gave me a clue about how she felt.

We went on a second date and it was equally as pleasant as the first, if not better. We were already more comfortable with each other—towards the end, I got a smooch and we held hands. I was on cloud-nine the entire time, and it's important to note that this was the first week I had gone without getting trashed in a long time— maybe even SINCE junior high.

That second date led to a third, then a fourth shortly after, and by the fifth date, I'd say we were full-on together. We had sex, and if either of us had any real friends, I'm sure we would've met them too. We brought up the past, prematurely mapped out a future, learned each other's insecurities, and bestowed trust. Needless to say, I was in love.

About six months in, I asked Christie to move in with me. She was reluctant at first, but excited by the prospect. I understand why she didn't immediately jump on it, though. Yeah, she had told me she loved me and all, but moving in together is a big deal for any couple. It could easily end up being a pivotal stage in the relationship, for better or worse.

Statistically, we weren't ready for that. But the hell with statistics, am I right? What do they know?

With fortuitous timing, Christie's landlord raised her rent, so I got my wish. She moved in with me instead of back in with her grandmother. We were about eight months in at that point—and probably unprepared, but whatever. I was still over-the-moon excited, and the day she moved in felt like one of the most important days of my life. I couldn't have been happier. And Christie shared that happiness with me, glad that she let go of her hesitancy.

I'm certain that feeling didn't stick around long for her.

Right before she moved in, Christie told me she had some conditions if she was going to stay with me. She told me that I could add anything if I wanted to, but I didn't have any. I was just satisfied we were finally going to live together. Christie would be, just as long as I followed some admittedly small requests.

Number one, and perhaps the biggest condition to me, was that she didn't want *any* drugs in our apartment. I hadn't done any in front of her for the first half of our relationship, but when I did, you'd think that she caught me shooting up in between my toes based off her reaction. All I did was take one Xanax—just one measly bar. Christie didn't exactly get angry; she became instantly worried about me as if I was going to O.D any second. I should have known not to take it in front of her though, and the fact that I did it so casually is a testament to how clueless I can be.

You see, while Christie knew my history with drugs—Cocaine, hallucinogens, and pills—she'd get antsy anytime the subject came up. And I knew why that was. Early on she had conveyed to me that both of her parents had died from drugs when she was around nine years old. That's how she came to live with her grandma just outside of the city, and since then she developed a disdain for drugs. Which, I totally understood and tried to respect. I never brought them up much, and I was doing less and less throughout our early relationship anyway. Sometimes I would even consider quitting them entirely, but I just couldn't commit. Luckily, Christie was willing to look past certain indulgences of mine.

The Xanax mishap was a different story. She was damn-near frantic about it, dude. From that point on, I was a little more careful about doing drugs around her. In a way I justified it to myself by suggesting she only got upset because she *saw* me take it. Which sounds like it doesn't make any sense, and I assure you, it doesn't. I was clearly enabling myself to keep getting fucked up, but in secrecy.

The second condition was that we meet each other's families before we officially announce that we're living together. Though in reality, that just meant meeting her grandma Debra. Any family I had was off limits, as my father was diagnosed with early onset dementia years before. Going to visit him at his assisted living community would've been pointless. Around the time I got out of high school, he was already having trouble recalling my face and name. Once I met Christie, I hadn't seen him in two years. Besides, my dad and I were never that close. As ironic and sad as it sounds, he wasn't the only one who felt he was conversing with a stranger the last time I talked to him.

Without my sick dad, runaway mom, and half siblings I don't give two shits about, my brother Jordan was the only person she had to meet on my side. Well, he was like a brother. We weren't actually family, so I guess it doesn't count, but he's been my best friend since the seventh grade. Or I guess I should say that he *was* my best friend. I'm sure he's cut ties with me since my arrest, if he hadn't already after the incident with his daughter...

Christie's family situation was somewhat similar. With her parents long gone, it was just her grandma. No siblings, important cousins, or even a grandfather. Debra was all she had, and looking at how it turned out, I'd say that Christie was all that Debra had as well.

So, just one little ole' lady and that's it. Seems simple enough, right? Yeah, that's what I thought, too.

We saved our meeting for Thanksgiving that year. But no matter how much preparation I had I was still nervous walking up to her door with a pumpkin pie in hand. I wondered in anguish if she was going to like me (she didn't) and I was also afraid she'd think I was bad for her granddaughter (I was).

This might be a little dumb to point out, considering they were related, but I was astonished how closely Christie and Debra resembled each other. When she opened the door, elated by her granddaughter's arrival, it was my first takeaway. My second was how tight of a bond they had.

The door swung open and a gasp followed. "Christie! Oh, my girl! You look so beautiful. If I had known that you were going to dress up, I would have at least put a bra on!" she crowed.

"Don't worry, Grandma!" She said in her embrace. "I'm not wearing one either."

Then they both cackled, almost in unison. Twas' a little creepy if I'm being straight up.

I tried to introduce myself. "Debra?" I stuck out my hand. "I'm Bra-"

"Guess what, Chrissy? I made that Oreo peanut butter pie you like!"

"I know you did! I wouldn't have come without it." She smirked. "How about the green bean casserole?"

"Well of course I made that. What do you take me for? Some kind of idiot?"

Christie giggled and once again wrapped her arms around her shortly. "Never *you*, Grandma. Oh, and this is my boyfriend, Brady."

Grandma Debra barely glanced my way and stuck her hand out. "Debra Peterson."

I shook her hand gently (before she pulled away within a second) and then we all went inside after her 'warm' welcome.

Debra was nice enough to me that day—in the most impolite way possible—but it'd be more accurate to say she wasn't a straight up bitch. She was only partly one. But that's not important. What's of value here is how I spent my time at Debra's and what I saw. Months later, it would be all I thought about for days.

Her house was the obvious residence of a hoarder. Clutter and dust covered nearly every square inch of her living room; I couldn't fathom it at first. Her house resembled a roadside antique shop from how tightly packed together everything was. There wasn't a single sign of organization.

The walls didn't have much available space either. If it wasn't a large painting of a picturesque landscape, it was antique café signs, personal photos, or uncolored photos of old Hollywood. Excluding Van Gogh's *The Starry Night* and a photo of a young Marlon Brando, I didn't recognize any of it.

Trying to play it cool and pretend like I was interested, I literally examined every single fucking thing hanging in that woman's living room. I guess I was curious, maybe a little, but mostly I was trying to seem attentive.

As I scanned all the personal and decorative photos on her wall, I came across something that made me double take. Originally, I thought it was some kind of black film reel, but I was way off. Next,

I thought it might be some sort of logo for something, and come to find out (months later) I was spot on.

It was about the size of a plate and had a carved center where it was empty in some areas. Kind of like a pretzel. While staring at it, I couldn't really pinpoint what it was made out of. At first glance I thought it was made of steel, then my next guess was rubber. But when I finally touched it, I gathered that it was definitely made out of wood; just painted black. It was a legitimate carving. The real deal. Whomever had made it even thoroughly sanded it down to be smooth to the touch. The round shape of the carving was only that—the shape. It was the frame to the center piece. And what the center was depicting, I still have no idea.

Eh, maybe I do have SOME idea. It's just a guess though. The center held either a tall tree, or an unrealistically lanky man. A part of me thought it could be a bug, too. Whatever it was, I was mesmerized by it, the craftsmanship being so precise yet ambiguous held my eyes captive.

But then I was called into the kitchen and left it. I never even asked Christie or her grandma what it was because I had quickly forgotten about it. I wonder what she would've said if I asked? Did Christie even know?

We spent all day at Debra's and when it was time to head out, I practically raced out of her house. Which, in retrospect, was probably not a good look.

I even left my jacket behind.

Being in a relationship is a lot of hard work—especially if you're in one with me. I think I've cheated on almost every girlfriend I've had, one way or another. And I usually start to harbor bad feelings towards them about half a year into dating. After that, it's only a matter of time until they receive my inconsiderate break-up text when I'm conveniently out of town.

Christie, of course, was the exception.

I didn't cheat on her, I didn't start to resent her after six months (more like a year) and breaking up via text would've been tricky since we lived together. But fortunately, I didn't need to break up with her. Nope, Christie did me a solid there. She was the one who pulled the plug on us. Either that or our relationship just ran out of time and expired.

That's kind of a stretch, though. At the time it certainly seemed like our dynamic as a couple imploded, but that's likely me sharing the blame. I know it was my behavior that had warped what was once a fruitful relationship.

When we passed our year mark, she started to constantly accuse me of being high. She'd say things like 'Why are your pupils so big, Brady? Or 'Why are you so jittery?' or my least favorite, 'Why can't you get your dick hard?' Don't judge me; coke-dick is a real thing. It's very similar to whisky-dick, but totally unlike Andy-Dick. I feel like every time she asked, she already knew I was, but that didn't stop me from fighting it each time. I'd deny, deny, deny until she would forfeit.

Then came a day where she came home early and saw me doing rails off her laptop.

As you could guess, she was livid. And this led to a HUGE fight, but with an unforeseeable ending.

I don't know if she was trying to sneak up on me or what but I didn't hear her open the door. I was leaned over, collecting a line of booger sugar with my sniffer. I was also sucked into *Goodfellas* playing on the TV, and now that you know that, you might understand why I was doing blow in the middle of the day.

Without any hint of her entrance, she rushed into our living room. The back of our couch was facing the door and once she saw me snorting, Christie didn't waste another second.

"What the fuck, Brady? You can't be serious! This is what you do when I'm not home?" Her eyes were tearful in a millisecond. (Goddamn actress.)

I shot up to my feet and attempted to defend myself. "Christ-babe-, Oh-I- I didn't think you'd be home so soon." Not my best defense, I'll admit.

"How long have you been lying to me? Did you EVER quit?"

"Of course, I quit! This is just a one-off thing, baby. Someone gave me this shit."

Calling my bluff, she peered past me and saw a decent sized bag of cocaine. It didn't take a DEA agent to know that it wasn't a 'free sample' amount. It was also clear that I couldn't snort all of it in one night even if I wanted to.

"I can't trust anything you say! Honestly, why would I, Brady? Tell me. I can't even believe I let someone like you drag me along like this."

"Someone like me? Come on, Chrissy, just take it easy. It's not the end of the world. I'm not gonna kill myself with it."

"Yeah, I'm sure my parents thought the same thing, Jackass."

Frustrated with the constant comparison, I fired back. "Your parents were HEROIN junkies, Christie! I've never even touched that stuff."

"You know what?" She scoffed. "I can't deal with this right now." Then she turned her back to me and fled the living room.

"Chrissy, what are you doing?" I tailgated her to our bedroom. My heart was running miles in my chest from the coke as well as the fight, so I was on her ass like a tick.

"Get away from me and don't call me that! I'm packing a bag and leaving. I don't want to look at you if you're tweaking like this."

"*Tweaking?* Will you stop being so dramatic for once? This isn't Second City."

"Second City is for comedy! God, you are such a dick! And so what if I'm being dramatic? My parents are fucking dead because of loser-shit like that! Fuck you, Brady! You knew exactly how I feel about that stuff."

Pacing around our room now, I started to get angry. "Oh, save it. Just listen to yourself! So fucking high and mighty. Who are you to judge? There are MILLIONS of people who have happily done cocaine and lived to tell the tale. Why do you think people keep doing it, huh? It's because the stories are AWESOME!"

She ignored my defense and continued packing.

I took a breath and went with a different tone. "Chrissy girl, I love you, but sometimes you make me feel like a giant piece of shit for something I just like to do occasionally… It's like you yell at me because you can't yell at your parents. You have to understand that I'm not them."

After grimacing at me, she stopped packing for a moment and then gazed into her bag. Then, as angrily as possible, she shoved it off the bed.

"I need you to go."

"Are you still leaving the apartment?"

"I don't know yet, but I want you to. I want to be alone. So, go."

"It's freezing outside. Where do you want me to go?"

"I don't care. Just leave."

I did what she asked and bailed. Before leaving I snagged my baggy and hit the streets until I was told to come back.

Wandering, and rolling hard, I was almost certain that we'd break up. I had the vivid image in my head of returning to our apartment, only to see all of her belongings were gone. Truthfully, the idea of it tore me apart then. I felt as if I had messed up a good thing.

Close to an hour and a half later, Christie texted my phone. I think it said something like "Where are you? Can you come back so we can talk?"

I hadn't strayed too far away from our building so within fifteen minutes, I was back home. In my mind, though coke-ridden, there were only two outcomes that awaited. One, we broke up, or two, I'd (unlikely) commit to getting off drugs and we'd stay together. Regardless of the outcome, I was just glad she was willing to talk.

I walked through our apartment door and it was dark all around. Christie hadn't bothered turning any of the lights on since the sun had gone down. The only hint of light was coming from our bedroom. A little taken off guard, I approached our closed-over door slowly and peaked in.

She was on her stomach, candles on the nightstand and at two corners of the room. It smelt like a bakery inside, but looked even sweeter. Christie was stark naked.

With her hair tied in a bun, I could make out the definition of her back; the divot of her spine leading down and stopping in between the two dimples above her ass, and the trio of tiny moles on her shoulder that made a triangle if you were to draw a line from each one. From my angle at the door, I could also see her boobs being pressed against the bed as she lay on them. A sight that I used to cherish.

I knocked on the door once, opening it further. "Christie? You still mad?"

I was at the foot of the bed, and at the sound of my voice, she put her butt in the air briefly and then put her knees beneath her chest. Sitting in child's pose, she eventually sat up and shook her head at me.

"No, not so much. But I've been thinking."

"Yeah? Well, you should hear what I'm thinking right now." I said, hoping I could put my money where my mouth was and actually achieve a boner—I had just taken two key bumps before walking in.

She giggled, this time in a genuine way. I was PSYCHED to hear it.

"Tell me what you were thinking about?"

She hesitated, then made eye contact and spilled it. "I think I want to try some. Maybe just this once."

"Try what?"

"You know... Come on, don't make me spell it out for you."

"No? I don't think I do…?"

"*Jesus…* The *coke*, Brady. I want to do some with you."

I was floored. I couldn't even believe she referenced cocaine without a spiteful tongue. In my coked-up head, I briefly suspected that it was some sort of sting operation I was the center of. I thought that, maybe, a desperate maverick cop had bribed my hot girlfriend and set me up…But I knew that didn't make any sense. It just seemed more likely than Christie suddenly doing rails with me.

She wasn't bullshitting though, Christie and I did coke all night and fucked like it was the eighties. She *loved* it, too. No surprise there. Christie continued to do it with me for the rest of our time together and our whole dynamic changed. We became this adventurous and experimental couple that I never envisioned for us before. To say it was a change of pace would be a major understatement; we were in a completely different race at that point.

And THEN we broke up.

I'm not proud to admit this, but she had every right to walk out on me. I pretty much forced her. I became restless in the relationship; nothing could have made me happy or content. And instead of breaking up with her directly like a man, I had her do all the heavy lifting.

I picked fights at every corner of conversation. Found something wrong with literally everything she did and especially fought her on what made her happy. I even belittled her passion and dream for acting by saying heartless stuff like, "If it really mattered to you, you wouldn't be in fucking Chicago. You'd be in California. Quit kidding yourself and move on." Or, I'd say stuff about the state of our relationship like "I had sex more often as a single man than I do with you. What do you think that says about us?" You know, just petty and cruel things that would make anybody want to leave.

Truth is, none of the shit I nitpicked about her actually mattered to me, but it was as if I tricked myself into believing that it did. Though in reality, I was just hoping she'd pick up and leave my ass. Which she did, just so we're clear. After a huge drug-induced fight and me leaving the apartment because of it, she packed up in a hurry and moved out with little to no notice.

And just like that, it was over, but when I say that, I really mean **far from over**.

III

Adrianna. Smithers. Condolences.

I moved to Chicago shortly after I turned twenty-one and within my first week there, I met Adrianna Brown and Blake Smithers. They went on to be practically the only people I'd see or talk to on a regular basis during my seven years in the city. With that being said, I still wouldn't say they were *real* friends.

While Adrianna and I got along all right, we were exclusively fuck-buddies and that's it. That's likely the only reason we ever got along in the first place; because we thoroughly used each other and didn't lie about it. We weren't looking to date, hangout, or learn about each other. Our dynamic just consisted of using each other for friction. I always believed that we had similar libidos, and because of that our sexual chemistry was addictive and honed early on. I've done things with Adrianna that I don't even feel comfortable writing down. I'm halfway shocked that she never made me sign an NDA. Actually, come to think of it, I should've had her sign one just for safe keepings.

Our 'partnership' had endured four of her boyfriends and three of my past girlfriends. But no worries, we never intruded on each other's relationships. We respected the fact that one of us was in love—or trying to be—and we usually kept our distance. By the time I got with Christie, Adrianna had been dating some dude for almost a year, but they eventually split midway into Christie and I's duration together.

Unlike Adrianna, I never went without seeing Blake Smithers. I was always in need of his services, and that's exactly what he provided: A service. Adrianna and I might've been 'buddies' in a certain way, but I can confidently say that Smithers and I weren't pals in any shape or form. To him, I was nothing but a longtime customer.

To be clear, I never actually wanted to be Blake's friend—or Smithers, as he preferred to be called. He was callous, stoic, and kind of intense. You wouldn't think that a drug dealer would be such a Debbie-Downer, but that's pretty much what he was. This one time I called him Blake after picking up and he was quick to correct me. "Aye, quit calling me Blake, bruh. Call me Smithers. Like the bad boss dude in *The Simpsons*... Ain't nobody in this motherfucker callin' me Blake—the fuck?"

I didn't challenge it. I just obliged and called him Smithers from then on out—even though 'Smithers' isn't who he thinks it is in *The Simpsons*. He was referring to Mr. Burns, Homer Simpson's cruel boss. Smithers was Mr. Burn's meek servant. But I didn't have the heart—or the balls—to tell him that. I needed to stay on his good side. Not only was Smithers shady as can be, he was also my only plug. I used to get all my pills from him, as well as my blow, my hallucinogens, and even weed when I rarely wanted it. The dude had the deals, too. I used to joke that he was like the Wal-Mart of drug dealers, with his rewarding prices and wide selection. He never laughed though.

Regardless, he was sketchy as hell. Smithers was always mean muggin' and rolling off something when I saw him. He was also decked out in crude tats from head to toe. None of which had any real meaning; like the baked T-rex with red eyes on his shoulder blade, or the shabby blue trailer illustrated on his forearm. I realize that being covered in tattoos doesn't automatically mean someone is bad news, but it certainly didn't help Smithers appear anymore friendly.

This one time he got to meet Christie. Well, 'meet' might be a little bit of a stretch. We were picking up some Xanax and she came inside with me, which I'm sure she regretted as soon as we walked in. The guy gawked at her as if I had just walked in with fucking Angelina Jolie. It immediately unsettled Christie, and she was sure to voice that to me on the way out.

I'm not sure what she expected though. Christie was even the one who insisted on coming in with me. She had said, "I wanna see where we're getting this stuff if I'm putting it in my body." As if that was going to make her feel better about it. Meeting a drug dealer is like meeting the guy who flips patties at

Sonic; it doesn't make the drugs or the burger any better, and half the time they're the same guy anyway.

Both Adrianna and Smithers unknowingly carried me through the break-up. Smithers, with his deals on downers, and Adrianna, with her sexual confidence and lack of gag reflex. Without their skills and services, it would have been near impossible for me to persevere. I saw them a lot after Christie fled. Adrianna more than Smithers.

Although she had felt for my break up, she was ecstatic that we were going at it again. I could tell she was eager the first time we hooked up. She took full advantage of the fact that I was still reeling from Christie and I's relationship. We brought in toys, filmed ourselves, and eventually exhausted each other's bodies. In spite of that, Adrianna never knew when to call the quits.

Even though I had been single for about a month, I had hardly spent any time alone. Adrianna was typically over at my apartment or I was over at hers. And while I appreciated her being around, it was starting to feel like I hopped out of one relationship just to get into another. Adrianna and I weren't even close to being in love, though the amount of time we spent together made it seem like we were *trying* to be. But as I reflect on this now, I'm beginning to think that she was merely mourning over her own collapsed relationship by spending that much time with me…Or maybe she was just horny. I don't know for sure. Adrianna had always been somewhat of a nympho since I met her, so it's hard to say.

Nevertheless, I felt that we were in too deep with each other. I mostly wanted to sleep with other women, but I also wanted just a little bit of alone time. With how fast Adrianna and I jumped into it, I had barely mourned over my own break up. Since we separated, I'd been too consumed with pills and pussy to even know how I felt about losing her. I wondered how it all affected Christie, too...

Adrianna agreed to taking a break without any resentment. Honestly, she even seemed a little excited about holding off. She claimed that "It's just going to make it *soo* much hotter when we fuck again!" I couldn't argue with that logic, but that wasn't my intention. And part of me believes she only accepted a break because she thought it was a new kink or a challenge. She even sent me a nude the same day.

Right after I broke the news to Adrianna, I hit up Smithers as well. A week or so without sex was one thing, but I was still going to need something to keep me occupied.

When Christie and I were together, I stayed away from psychedelics. Which, frankly, surprised me because I started tripping when I was like fifteen and

I *loooved* it right from the start. I was almost passionate about taking acid and eating shrooms. And truthfully, I've never have had what you would call a 'bad trip'. I was all about the laughter it brought on, the way your cheek bones feel sore from smiling, and even the wavy lines and tracers were a blast. But no matter how often I praised hallucinogens, Christie wanted no part of it. And once she was gone, I was stoked to finally take them again.

Christie was terrified of tripping because she once read that it could evoke any underlying mental disorders a person has. I'm not totally sure if that's accurate or not, but if you heard how many times she expressed concern for her mental state because of her mother's struggle with being a borderline personality, you'd understand why she was so wary of hallucinogens. And then you would also understand why I resisted tripping while dating her. Getting lectured while high on shrooms or acid is the WORST.

Say what you want about drug dealers, but it can still be a demanding gig. Like any job you had the professionals, and the not-so-professionals. Fortunately for me, Smithers was the former. He responded to my text about shrooms and told me to pull through.

Smithers somehow could afford his own house not too far from the city, but despite it being in a decent neighborhood, it might as well have had "COCAINE SOLD HERE." advertised on his lawn. Some of his windows were cracked, his gutter was hanging off the house and touching the ground, the white paint appeared ashy, and he hardly ever mowed the grass. How everyone else in his neighborhood was okay with living next to a conspicuous drug dealer was beyond me, but each time I left, I was certain that it wouldn't be long until police kicked in his door. Yet I never failed to return and put myself in that position.

That day, like any, I wanted to be in and out of Smithers house. Thankfully he had it weighed and ready to go when I got there, but I still ended up lingering in his living room. He didn't let me leave as quickly as I wanted.

There was something strikingly different about him. He seemed... nicer, I guess. Upon walking into his place, he told me that there was some extra in my sack and when I went to dap him up, he nearly hugged me. It wasn't a tight embrace or anything, but it was still unordinary. Smithers wasn't that kind of guy. He didn't concern himself with making you feel welcome nor did he care if you ever came back.

Ignoring his drastic change in demeanor, I forked over the cash and turned to dart out.

And that's when I first heard any hint of the news.

In a bashful, partly awkward tone, he said. "Aye, bro, I just wanted to say condolences by the way."

Condolences?

Condolences for what?

IV

Overdid it'.

All right, here comes the bad part. Actually, no, I take that back—all of it was bad, but this might've been the worst solely because of how it made me feel. It hurt back then, and it still does now. Until then, I had never felt so much regret. Although NONE of this would've happened if I hadn't met Christie, this is precisely when my plummet to rock bottom started. I wanna say that I wasn't aware of that then, but subconsciously, I think I was. The news demolished me like a hit from a speeding mac truck.

When Smithers dropped his condolences on me, I didn't react much. I just said "Thanks, bro," and bailed. But he did succeed in lighting a curious fuse for me. The whole drive home I was trying to guess what he had meant. Once I made it back to my apartment, I started investigating. First, I tried Facebook. I didn't know exactly what I was looking for, but it didn't take me but five minutes to find it. With just a few name searches, I knew why Smithers had offered his condolences.

I admittedly didn't think to search Christie's name at first because she blocked me right after the break up. Therefore, I hadn't heard anything from or about her since she moved out about a month ago. Not a single message; not an I miss you, I still love you, or even a fuck you. She was done with me. Before I learned the truth, I thought she was just sticking to her guns.

But while getting to the bottom of my drug dealer's sympathy, I ran out of names early on. Smithers only knew the bare minimum about me. Just what I allowed him to see. How could he have known who I was close to? And if he did, how did he hear about their passing before I heard?

Then it dawned on me.

Already sure of the result, I looked up Christie's full name, and just like that, it was all clear.

I found a new profile using her name, but when I clicked on it, the entire layout was different from the typical Facebook profile. It looked more like a business page rather than a personal one. Her profile picture was a recent photo she had taken—one I've never seen—and there was a red banner across the bottom.

The banner read: **Remembering Christie D'Angelo.**

Someone had turned it into a hashtag. From top to bottom, the page was filled with heartfelt and mournful posts about Christie. Most of which used the hashtag to sign off with.

I read a lot of them, tears in my eyes and in disbelief. Throughout reading, I was ashamed that I'd never heard of any of the people mourning Christie. They all seemed to know her fairly well. Some were around our age, likely from Chicago's theater community. Others were clearly family— strangely all women.

One lady, who happened to be a silver fox with the same enticing eyes as Christie, shared a post mentioning her grandmother.

My sweet Chrissy, I just got off the phone with Debra, and I'm still reeling from what she told me...This has to be some sort of nightmare. Please, call me and tell me it isn't true...Is our little Bette Davis gone? I hate that I know it to be true... Christie

Marie, you were the most generous and gorgeous gift our family has ever received. We love you and miss you so much already. Your Grandma is having a hard time, but I think she'll overcome her grief. She just needs your help.

Rest in Paradise, baby girl.

The reality of her death began to sink in with every post. I remember trying to vaguely convince myself it was all a misunderstanding. As if everyone on the page was remembering a different Christie D'Angelo despite all the similarities. But it was her, I couldn't play *that* stupid. And the more I accepted it, the more I wanted to kick my own ass. I couldn't believe that I let her die, even if we were already broken up. I took the blame right from the start, and that was before I even discovered the blame already belonged to me.

What happened didn't initially click for me. Out of respect, none of the top posts had come out and said it. I had some slim guesses but nothing I truly believed in. At first, I assumed she had been involved in a fatal car accident. Only problem with that was the fact that Christie didn't drive. My next guess was that she'd been straight up MURDERED. I write that in all caps because it seems silly to me now. Christie wasn't murdered by some maniac in the streets. Of course, people did get murdered in Chicago, but suggesting something that heinous happened to Christie? Unreal. Although, at the same time, that's probably how everyone feels when it comes to murder and someone they love.

The cause of death should've been obvious, especially to me of all people. The blood was practically on my hands. Nevertheless, I still had to dig for the answer.

I googled her name, hoping an article, report, or obituary would appear. Nothing had though. So, I was back on Facebook.

Scrolling through dozens of wordy posts and old photos on her remembrance page, I eventually found an answer. The man who posted it was a spitting image of Peter Parker—yes, Spider-Man, but before the bite. So, I guess he was just a nerd with brown hair. Anyway, he shared a post that was a little more revealing than others.

Leading with a photo of Christie and him in the middle of a scene on stage, both wearing hobo-like clothing, it read:

Devastated. 🙁 *We weren't close, but I always thought you were exceptionally talented and painfully funny. I loved every minute of acting with you and I adored our group trips to IHOP after a show. Your life was cut far too short, anybody that knew you knew that you had a promising future ahead, and to hear it's been ripped away from you is nothing but cruel and unfair. We'll miss you, Christie. You're irreplaceable.*

He wasn't finished just yet though. Apparently ole' Rick Moranis wanted to separate himself from the other mourners even more.

Let this be a crude reminder that it could happen to anyone…If you know someone struggling with addiction, don't be afraid to talk to them about it. Ask if they need help…You could end up saving a life.

#RememberingChristieD'Angelo

V

Earshot. Microdosing. Target

When I was a kid, likely no older than seven, my dad told me we were going all-out for a camping trip that summer. We'd been camping many times before, but we usually went somewhere fairly local. That year, he wanted to do some brief traveling.

His enthusiasm for a summer excursion wasn't inspired by me though. Around this particular time, he had started dating a younger woman, and to impress her, he rented a luxurious cabin at the lake of Ozarks! I have a feeling that he might've told her that he *owned* the cabin, but either way, I was extremely excited. I had never been out of the state by then. And until we arrived, I thought it was in store to be the highlight of my summer.

Our trip also aligned with the Fourth of July, so that made things even more memorable. We picked up some fireworks on the way—at a legitimate store for fireworks. It wasn't a tent like I was used to back in Illinois. The building was the size of a grocery store and mostly sold explosives, but also liquor and fancy types of cigarettes. Evidently Missouri is a little more lenient with explosives and substances that make explosives that much more desirable.

Despite how excited I was to go to a renowned lake for vacation, I was a tad bitter about staying in a cabin. My dad lived life as an outdoorsman, but the bratty woman he was shacking up with refused to camp somewhere without air conditioning or a personal shower. Which, for the record, shouldn't be considered camping… At that point you're just staying in an outdoorsy hotel.

She got her way, though, and my dad soon encouraged me to drop my snarky comments about it. He reassured me by saying "Cabin or not, we're still in for a good time, bub. Just give it a chance, you'll see. And the cabin is only for sleeping anyway, Brady! We'll be outside more than anywhere else."

Like any naïve seven-year-old would, I believed him. But when we arrived at the two-bedroom cabin, my dad and his girlfriend went inside, and didn't come back out until it was time to head home. I only saw his girlfriend leave their room once the entire time we were there. She tip-toed out bottomless in my dad's T-shirt then grabbed a bottle of rum and a melon before returning to the bedroom. She didn't even see me watch her do it. The woman was too consumed with her all-paid vacay to notice me. Can't blame her.

So, while my dad was getting his rocks off with her and a cantaloupe, I was outside most of the time. On the actual day of the fourth, I had found some kids nearby to hang out with. They were cool enough—though it was obvious they were a little more country oriented or hickish than myself. I imagine they were born and bred Missourians from the sticks. Most of their parents were outside with us, but they were drunk off their asses. Like my dad's girlfriend, I doubt if they even noticed me. They sure as hell weren't paying attention to any of their own children.

Later in the evening when things were picking up firework-wise, me and this kid, Travis, broke off from the rest of the group. He was a year older than me, but we had a little more in common—we both cursed up a storm in private and loved Limp Bizkit. I guess both of our dads had been fans and we had similar stories on how we jacked their CDs. I found mine in my dad's car in a leather disc case and Travis found his copy in his dad's garage/gym.

Repeating all the adult things we once heard Fred Durst spit, we meandered down to the lakeside to shoot off our collective fireworks. We shot roman candles into the water and at each other, blew up firecrackers underneath our shoes, threw smoke bombs as far as we could, and drew in the air with kiddy sparklers; all while reciting lyrics we didn't understand. I can even distinctively remember what he was rapping when he found the glass bottle.

"I won't lie, that I can't deny, I did it for the nookie! Come on—the nookie! Come on—the nookie! And stick it up your c- oh hey! Check it out, dude. I found something that we can blow up." he excitedly claimed, showing me a dirty wine cooler bottle with cigarette butts at the bottom. "Tie some of them bobcats together and I'll drop 'em inside."

I did as he asked. I took about six of my firecrackers and twisted their wicks together. To be real, I was just as into the idea as Travis was. It seemed harmless, yet thrilling and irresponsible. *Huh? What's that? You want to blow up glass where children play barefoot? COUNT.ME.IN.* What the hell were we thinking? Reckless little bastards.

He walked with the bottle and placed it several feet away from where we were going to stand. At first it seemed like a decent enough distance, and I was right. It would've been totally safe; if he stayed by me and had been patient. Or just smarter in general.

Travis took the twisted bobcats and maneuvered them into the bottle. Once he got them in but still had a hold of the entangled wicks, he lit them with his handy lighter. Side note: Travis, who was probably in the third grade, had full access to a BIC lighter. Not a punk, but an actual lighter. His parents even removed the child's safety for him! No wonder things turned out like they had.

Anyway, it didn't explode like we expected it to. After about a minute, we both thought the firecrackers were duds or got wet at the bottom.

Frustrated, Travis stomped over to the piece of glass-trash and picked it up. His next move seemed unsafe, even then. I guess he was wanting to hear if the wick was still burning.

Dude didn't even think twice about it.

He put the lip of the bottle to his ear and *BOOM!*

Fragments of glass tore open the side of his face. Blood gushed from his shredded ear and his lobe dangled from the wound like cheese from a hot and sloppy slice of pizza. A shard of glass protruded out of his left eyeball, revealing just how gushy and soft the eye actually is; it looked like penetrated Jell-O. Right away Travis yelped then screamed. I stared, petrified and lightheaded while his parents rushed over. I'm not sure how far away they were, but I fainted before they reached us.

And that's precisely when I learned that I don't do well around blood. Any sight of gore is like an instant flu to me. From that day on, my dad gently teased me about being squeamish.

Given that I was late in finding out about Christie, I missed her funeral. On one hand it depressed me, but on the other, I knew I wouldn't have been welcome there. I was a culprit to her demise, whether she had loved me or not. I suspected Grandma Debra at least felt that way.

Even though I blamed myself for what happened, I knew there wasn't much that could be done. She was dead. What was I supposed to do about it? Mope around and wish things hadn't panned out like they did? No thanks. I did that for about half a week, of course, but I snapped out of it. I had things to tend to, like the shrooms I purchased before finding out.

Naturally I put off tripping. I wasn't in the right headspace while mourning, and a bad trip, like always, was unwanted. Plus, as mentioned, I was stoked to take mushrooms again, so it was hard to smother the hankering I had for hallucinogens. I was ready to trip-out. I wanted to stare at the moon and laugh my ass off, or take some time to appreciate how soft my carpet is because I'm so high that I need to sit. For some reason, I felt I deserved that.

Surprisingly, as often as I've tripped, I had never microdosed with shrooms before. I wanted to try it, though. Overtime people have told me that the trip goes by way smoother but it's just as fun. On top of that, they'd mention how it's a good way to expand your experience a little. I think that's what sold me. With that in mind, my plan was to trip from sunrise to sundown with a little over an eighth of mushrooms.

If you've never taken mushrooms, you should know that despite being 'magic', they taste like burnt pumpkin seeds that were hidden up someone's butt. Don't let anybody else tell you differently. I usually gag when scarfing down a handful or two, but this time, I started with two *pinches*. And prior to that, I was sure to eat a decent breakfast. Last thing I wanted was a tummy ache to crush my high. No one wants to sit on the toilet for half an hour while tripping sack—your butt gets SO sweaty. It's like those mid-shower dumps when you have to hop out and sit your soaking wet ass on the toilet.

My plan for that day was simple. After some breakfast and two (or three) doses, I intended on hanging out at home and coming up slowly. When an hour or so went by I'd take more, then I was going to grab some lunch and see a movie afterwards. At the end, I wanted to come down with a pleasant walk at Northly Island Park.

I almost made it, too.

Well, not really. I got as far as lunch.

The initial pinches I ate must've been the most potent because it hit me hard. Don't get me wrong, I felt great; I just wasn't expecting to be that high by noon. I ended up getting distracted by my fishtank and how dirty my bathroom was, and before I knew it, it was almost two. I missed my showtime. I can't remember what I was seeing that day, but it was supposed to start at one-thirty.

It didn't ruin my plans entirely, though. All I had to do was find a different flick at a different time, and I'd be set. But if that was the plan, I needed to get moving so I readied myself. Leaving my place, I ate three (four) more pinches and ventured into the city. But not before I ran back inside my apartment and ate two more pinches. (As you can tell, I wasn't very good at microdosing.)

For lunch I went to McDonalds. The man at the register appeared to know I was zoinked out of mind from how big he smiled at me. Or that's just what I told myself anyway. He could've just been happy. Either way, it freaked me out and I panicked while ordering. I ended up getting a cheeseburger happy meal with apple slices and a coke.

At a table far from the rest of the customers, I devoured my tiny burger with my head down, then tossed the apples and headed back out. Somehow, I found another showtime and was committed to making it, but there was a problem ensuing. All the noise, people, and paranoid thoughts were getting to me. I began to fear that everybody was making comments about the way I looked or the way I behaved. I had become certain that the McDonalds cashier had told everyone I was tripping. And it also didn't help that I saw my eyes in a building's reflection on the street. My pupils were the size of marbles, dude. It was terribly apparent that I was high, and not in a whimsy, acceptable way either. It was more like a 'keep away from the man in the seven-eleven parking lot' high.

Afraid but still determined, I continued on and stopped by Target for some cheap movie snacks.

Inside the super market, I insisted on keeping my head down. The vibrance of the store was overwhelming. I hadn't stared directly up at the lights, but from how the white tiles reflected off of them, I felt like I had. Additionally, it was freezing inside and it reminded me of high school, which made me sad because I didn't graduate. I thought about how my dad was understandably disappointed in me for dropping out. Then I started thinking about him and how he practically lost his mind in his late forties. And that made me dwell over my own mental state, which, as you know, was pretty vulnerable at the moment.

That's how you think while on mushrooms. Any topic is a slippery slope. On the surface I was sorting through sour patch kids, but internally, I was wrestling with myself. And I was pretty sure I was losing. Nevertheless, my perilous thoughts while tripping are irrelevant here. It's what happened next that's notable.

I needed to leave Target because my showtime was approaching. Thankfully, they had the self-checkout stations up and running. That was huge to me because I was fairly certain I couldn't speak without sounding terrified.

I found an available station, scanned my candy and soda, then ran my card to pay. In the brief period when the machine was processing my card, my eyes bravely wandered. And it didn't take them long to find something to marvel at.

There was a girl looking at me, about ten to fifteen feet away from me at a normal register.

I'd say she was in her late teens or early twenties. She was working that particular lane, but there were no customers waiting. Instead of playing on her phone like most cashiers would do during downtime, she was just gazing at me. Her eyes on me alone were frightening thanks to the shrooms, but her unfortunate appearance made it a million times worse.

Most of the skin on her face was missing.

In some areas it was more severe than just missing skin. The girl didn't have one of her cheeks intact. I could see her molars through her open right side. The impression her deformities gave me was that she had been in a serious accident or barely escaped a house fire as a child. All in all, I didn't have a clue what happened to her, and even more so, I didn't know why she was staring. I recall thinking it was somewhat cruel to even have her working the register, given the gawks she likely received from customers…just like how I was staring at her.

However, she didn't seem to mind me looking. In fact, she seemed to be into it. She twirled her auburn hair flirtatiously, smiled at me and even twinkled her thin fingers my way as a wave. I was appalled by her confidence. While glad she didn't live bashfully, I was utterly disturbed by her peeled face reveling in the attention.

My card went through—after what seemed like an hour—and I got the hell out of there. My hands were shaking, the hair on my body stayed standing well after, and I fought the urge to be sick. After that I ditched the movie and went straight home. The cashier's face and flirty eyes was I could think about. I was even afraid that she followed me on the way home.

I reached a point where I began to wonder if she was real. Maybe it was just the shrooms? They were hallucinogens, after all. You're supposed to see things to a certain degree…right?

But no matter how hard I tried to convince myself of that, I never bought it. No one trips *that* hard. Not in public anyway. That's some *Fear and Loathing* shit. Which is supposedly a true story, so never mind. I guess people do trip that hard in public.

But not me! I'm not Hunter S. Thompson. I didn't eat enough shrooms for that. I don't think anybody could. There's no way I imagined her. Her scars were unique, and her smile was too genuine to be an illusion. I've never had the imagination to conjure something that detailed.

That girl was as real as fireworks are dangerous.

They all were.

VI

Club-E. Some Strange. Wet.

I've been going to night clubs for years now. Or I did, before I wound up in the cuckoo's nest, that is. From eighteen to twenty-three I probably went the most in my life. In more recent years, I still went from time to time, but not nearly as often. I'm not sure why that is; maybe it was the decline of quality in today's music; maybe it was the price of drinks skyrocketing. Who knows.

Either way, I went less and less in my mid to late twenties. Christie and I never went clubbing together, and after our break-up—and her overdose—I only went once. It was my very last time, and for good reason.

What ended up being my final night at the club was set for the Saturday after my miserable mushroom trip. The plan was inspired by an ad I saw the next morning after zero rest. Sleep was unattainable after microdosing and recalling the cashier's nasty scars all night, but despite my exhaustion, I felt wired and jumpy in the morning. Whenever I saw the ad on Facebook for a local club's anniversary party, I committed immediately.

In eccentric red font, the ad read: GREY GOOSE PRESENTS—CLUB EVOCAVTIVE'S FIFTEEN ANNIVERSARY BASH! FREE ADMISSION FOR SINGLE WOMEN. HALF PRICED DRINKS FOR ALL WOMEN. Men—$5-dollar entry.

Evocative—club-E for short—was a pretty lit spot. Fights were rare due to tight security, so it felt safe for everybody. The staff thrived under pressure, so the service at the bar was efficient. And on crazy nights, drunk chicks were known to take their tops off on the dance floor and kiss each other, which caused all the men to go straight bananas. Every.Single.Time.

However, as appealing as all that sounds, I think the most distinct part of club-E were the massive, blood-red lights that burned throughout the night. It was like going to a rave in a snake's cage, or rolling on ecstasy on Mars.

Getting laid was almost too easy there. Just about everyone gets wasted, and by the time the red lights cease and the plain, fluorescent lights come on around three a.m., people make haste decisions. And about half the time, it ends up being a regretful choice when sober. I've been on both sides of that spectrum, and every time, I preferred to be the one regretting. The other side just hurts your feelings.

Anyway, I planned to attend the anniversary bash a week ahead, completely oblivious to my condition and the fact that a club might be the worst place for me at that point and time.

Due to how rocky my mushroom trip had been, I decided to stay clean until the party. That meant no drinking, no tripping, no snorting, no popping, no nothing! I wanted my mind and body to have at least a week to recover before I inevitably went apeshit with cocaine and hard liquor.

Prior to my sentencing, I worked at a Toyota dealership. No, I didn't sell cars, if that's what you're picturing. I only cleaned and detailed them. To help keep my mind off certain vices, I picked up some extra hours. Fortunately, the week went by quick and without a snag. Clocking out on Friday, I hadn't expected a single thing. But that's precisely what's fucked up about that work week.

I had really believed everything was normal, even when there were tell-tale signs all around. I saw peculiarity, but I tried my hardest to ignore it. For just one example, my boss, Marge, a broad and stout middled aged woman who was too dour to laugh, kept grinning at me all week.

From her upstairs office window, she persisted with an abnormal smile, watching me scrub and clean. It got to the point where I avoided looking her direction at all. To diminish it, I just told myself she was messing with me—though I knew we didn't have that type of relationship. When I clocked out at the end of the week, I briskly walked by her office to leave. I had waited until she was occupied with a salesman to do so. I tried not to look inside, but ended up taking a glance. What I saw, I boiled down to several harmless explanations.

She had red stains all over her grey shorts, her entire crotch was covered with smearing on the legs. I only dwelled on it briefly; I hadn't even made it home by the time I brushed it off as an oil spill. About a week later, when I was starting to put together the pieces, I realized it was exactly what I first thought.

It wasn't oil or some other spill, it was blood.

One could accomplish a lot socially at Evocative. Sometimes you left with more friends than you came with, sometimes it was just contacts, a date, or just somebody to get trashed with next weekend. I'd like to say they counted as friends as well, but I had zero intention of ever hanging out with any of them on the outside. Most of the time I enjoyed their company solely from the alcohol in my system that night.

I only had one goal at the anniversary party, and that was to tame some strange. A week or so had

gone by since the last time I had sex with Adriana—
or anybody—and I realize that doesn't sound like a
long time, but for me, it was unusual. Earlier in this
journal, I expressed how 'I got around' but that's
putting it lightly. I was a full-fledged pussy-hound.
It's legitimately the only reason I went to night clubs
to begin with—like most men.

I managed to score some blow the day before the
party, which upped my chances of getting laid. I'm
not sure if you know this or not, but women who
regularly go to clubs fuckin' ADORE cocaine.
Seriously, you wouldn't believe what they'd do for a
line or two. You just pull out a little baggy and *BAM!*
Their makeup, perfume, and the tasteful, sexy outfits
they wear are revealed as nothing more than a
costume and they suddenly become crackheads. With
just one gesture, the uninterested woman you were
hitting on start to emulate Gollum as they beg for the
precious.

I wore mostly black that night. Some dark jeans as bottoms, no undershirt, and a black buttoned shirt with the long sleeves rolled up and the top left unbuttoned. Before leaving, I did some bumps, then admired myself in the bathroom mirror. In my humble opinion, I looked like a sleezy version of Jake Gyllenhaal with no money. It was perfect.

It usually takes my eyes a minute or two to adjust to Club E's glow. That's exactly why I B-line to the bar first thing—and because I want my liquor pronto. The lighting by the bar was a light blue, which contrasted nicely to the overbearing red. After ordering a double rum and coke, I surveyed the dance floor from the bar. Raving and rubbing underneath the crimson glare were throngs of women, dozens upon dozens, all appearing wild and willing.

More than a few girls checked me out at the beginning of the night. None of which struck me in any way that lasted. Yeah, they were cute and all, and

I did offer them a bump when they approached, but they looked too young for me. Thing about clubs is, despite having to be twenty-one to enter, about a quarter of the crowd is likely under. I'm not talking minors here, but definitely under twenty-one. And while they're legal, they're also annoying and clingy.

Not before too long I found myself rolling hard in the center of the crowd, dancing my ass off. I've never considered myself a good dancer, but that was okay because the majority of the people at night clubs aren't either. Everybody just humps and grinds. It's like a dry humping orgy—if it's a good club.

Club-E really pulled some numbers that night. Even the path to the smoking pad was clustered with droves of drunks; forget about the restrooms. And while in a big crowd, it's best to accept the fact that accidents do happen. Maybe you'll get pushed a little, maybe somebody will step on your foot by mistake, or perhaps a klutz will spill some of their drink on you. It's not a huge deal, shit happens, right? And additionally, everyone is too hot and inebriated to care anyway. I don't mean hot as in attractive either. I mean it in the sweating your balls off kind of way. Next to all the sweat you gather in a dancing crowd, a little bit of vodka on your shirt is pretty unnoticeable.

Originally, I believed that everyone at the club was extra rowdy that night and that's why I was so wet. My jeans were damp to the touch, and my shirt stuck to my body as if someone had thrown a full drink at me, though I'm certain no one had. I hadn't even bumped into anyone to cause a spill, nor did I piss someone off enough to chuck a beverage at me.

Nope, I did well with the ladies that night. Some would say that I did especially well. But me personally, I'd say I did strangely and alarmingly well. Looking back, I should've known something was amiss. I did okay with women ordinarily, though on that night, they swooned over me as if I was a celebrity. I was partly concerned they actually thought I was Jake Gyllenhaal.

I danced with almost a dozen women that night, but I only pursued one vivacious blonde in particular. We first met at the bar when I was collecting my fifth round. From her choice of apparel, I noticed her without any trouble. To go along with her soft seeming, silky straightened hair that reached past her shoulders, she wore, as best as I can describe, a dish towel for a shirt.

Although stylish, it had no shoulders and lacked a back. It was only wearable by a few thin strings behind; sort of like how a bikini top is tied. I'm sure it was an expensive piece of clothing, but that's not why I fancied her. If I'm being honest, it was the sole fact she was rocking the side-boob look. The side of a titty used to drive me nuts, okay? I was weak.

After more than a couple of key bumps, we danced a little, but at that point, we knew the club was closing soon. Our time on the dance floor concluded with her brazenly sliding her hand down my pants. She grabbed my shaft with a sweaty hand and rubbed her thumb across the head of my cock. Massaging it, she leaned into my left ear and whispered, *"Wanna take me to your place and cum on me?"* And we couldn't have left the club any faster after she said that. It worked on me like a charm. Shit, I was half surprised I didn't bust in her hand right there, and I didn't even know her name.

But little did I know that would be the last time a woman could truly turn me on.

We took an uber home and she practically blew me the whole way there—it's okay, the driver was Italian. He rose a fist in a Black Panther fashion whenever our eyes met in the rearview. He never said much, but I could tell he was proud of me.

I've never met a stranger so eager. Before I even had the chance to unlock my door, she slipped off her skimpy shirt and waited topless in the halls. Afraid we were causing a ruckus, I frantically but also drunkenly tried to get my door open before somebody saw the crazy topless woman I was with.

Once we were inside, we did some rails and she continued to undress in my kitchen. While my head was down, she darted into my unlit bedroom, butt naked and giggling. I heard her plop down on my bed. Whenever I approached my bedroom door, I could scarcely see her positioned ass up and face down, waiting. My jeans grew instantly. Following her lead, I took of my damp clothes and went for it. I didn't even bother with turning my bedroom light on.

I knew something was wrong almost immediately.

Fleetingly I ate her out from the back. She shivered with pleasure as my tongue made gentle contact with her clit; wetter by the second. After, I flipped the blonde on her back and scooted her bottom to the edge of the bed. Next, I put her legs near my shoulders, but when I grabbed ahold of her ankle, it felt like her skin was covered with a layer of wet leaves. Preoccupied, I slid whatever it was off—assuming it was just a piece of wet clothing.

Ignoring the signs, I preceded to fuck her. Within two to three minutes, I halted. She was impossibly wet; an obscure amount of fluid splashed with every pump. While it felt somewhat normal, it sounded like I was humping a large pile of mashed potatoes and with every thrust, my midsection got more and more drenched. Taking a step back, I noticed my face, stomach and hands were just as wet. I tried to reach a conclusion and not seem concerned, but her shrieks, moans and lustful encouraging were distracting.

"What're you doing? Put it back in! *Pleaseee*, I need it. I need your fat dick back inside. Don't stop!" she moaned.

"Um, yeah, you bet. I will. Just give me one second." I said calmly before heading to the switch.

On the way to the light, I could literally feel myself dripping. Yet I wasn't prepared for what the light would unveil. A part of me considered that it could be blood– it happens, but the amount debunked the idea. My worries that it could be something like that was quickly washed away.

Then it came back as soon as I saw my hand after flipping the light switch.

My hand didn't just have blood *on* it, it was coated, along with a layer of flimsy skin bunched up at my palms. The switch even had a spot of red on it now. Surprised but not yet nauseas, I looked down at my chest and found nausea there. It was covered in a slick dark red juice just as much as my hands were. The same with my legs and especially my penis.

Thunderstruck and dizzy, I slowly turned my head to the blonde. My mouth was forced agape and my knees trembled when my eyes found her. Not only was the lively blonde just as bloody, but she was totally gutted in my bed. Yet she was alive somehow, still moaning and seductively caressing her mangled body. Her tits were gone, only balled up flesh sat on her chest. Her legs were shed down near to the bone, and her rib cage was just as visible as the side of her breasts were earlier. It was as if I was staring at a slutty zombie.

Swallowing bile, I stared blankly. Appearing bewildered from my reaction, she got on her knees on top of my mattress, her intestines pooled around, meat following off her bones. Sweetly she said, "You okay? You better keep fucking me." She bit her lip then ran her bloody fingers through her hair. Right after, her left hand found her cheek and stalled there delicately. "Come here, I'll let you stick it in my ass." She snickered, and as if she were fragilely made of warm wax, the blonde dragged her cheek off when her hand slid down to her mutilated chest.

With a mouth full of vomit, I sprinted away and locked myself in the bathroom.

She quickly ran after me and knocked on the door when she reached it, insisting that I come back out.

"Hey! What's wrong? You cool? It's not me, is it? I thought you wanted it dirty. Just come back out, we don't even have to do anal if you're not into that."

When she started to hear me retch and puke into the toilet, her tone soured.

"*Oh*, fuck you! You piece of shit! I fucking knew you were gay; it's written all over you. You could have just told me, but thanks for leading me on! Your dick is tiny by the way!"

"Just get out of here! Please!" I hollered between gags.

Curled up next to the toilet seat while my heart thumped hard enough to see my chest heave, blood seeped underneath the door while she waited outside. I spent the next four hours there, too sick and too confused to leave. I'm not sure when she bailed as I never heard the front door open nor close after she stopped talking.

Embracing the chill of the bathroom's tile, I started to contemplate my sanity for the first time. Even then, I heavily considered that a psychosis had just begun. For hours I pondered over my excessive drug use over the years and what I must've done to my brain. Covered in blood or not, there wasn't a second when I actually considered all the gore in the bedroom to be real.

I knew whatever was happening, was only happening to me.

VII

Showers. Detox. Uncle Brady.

Before I get into the thick of my downfall, there's something more recent I'd like to share. Something that happened just a few hours ago. It sums up why I need to off myself in a nutshell; the perfect example. And the worst part is how often it occurs. Maybe once you've read it, you'll understand better. I think I can still get this across, but bear with me. My head is still reeling from falling.

So, patients typically shower jailhouse style at Chilton's—especially the criminally insane. The washroom is this muggy, spotless white area no bigger than a classroom, equipped with twelve showerheads attached to the surrounding walls. We're given about ten minutes to wash up, and while we do, there's a few guards and even a few staff usually close by.

Usually.

Needless to say, things went a little differently this afternoon.

I was already aware that a shower was in my near future, so I wasn't alarmed when Birdy came and fetched me from the common area. What did strike me as odd, however, was the fact I wasn't being escorted by any guards. It was only Birdy walking closely behind me with two towels draped over her shoulder.

Trying not to fret, I assumed the others would soon follow. Even though a private shower sounded nice on paper, the image of being alone in that wide white room worried me. I had grown accustomed to

showering with company. Never in my life did I
think that showering with a handful of men would
bring me peace, but when your freedom—and
sanity—are snatched away, it's easy to embrace the
familiar. Showering with the other male patients felt
no different than showering with a team as a
teenager—only without the insecurities. They all
made me feel safe...despite each of them being
lunatics.

Wetting my hair and temporarily impairing my
vision, I heard the washroom door creak open. I
chose not to look, trusting it was the others finally
joining me. Keeping my head directed at the wall I
continued lathering my body. Confident, I even
began to whistle in the warmth of the water. And
that's when Birdy cued in with her own whistle, the
cat-calling kind.

Then, she exclaimed. "*Dammmmn*, baby! You got a tight ass on ya! You been doing squats in your room or somethin'?"

I flung myself around and slammed my back against the wall, shielding my privates. Birdy was on the other side of the shower area, only a towel covering her voluptuous figure.

"Why are you in here?" I hissed, "Don't come any closer!"

"Oh, come on. Don't be like that, Brady. You ain't even seen the goods yet." she said, right before she allowed her towel to drop.

Birdy then sauntered around the room, feeling out the space. I struggled to find my next move as she did so. Averting my eyes seemed to be my only choice. Though even with my eyes pulled away from her, I wondered what part of her flesh was going to slide off first. Birdy's a filled-out gal, which meant she had layers and layers to peel before she was nothing but blood and bone.

"I'm going to scream for the guards if you don't leave right now." I threatened.

"*Mmm, oh my god, would you?* Use that sexy-ass voice you got, all raspy and shit. You'd be wasting your time though. I think they're all outside or eating…Speaking of eating; what about you? Are you hungry, Brady?"

I shook my head vehemently, my chest heavy and my head feeling light. My heartbeat was in my ears, and my eyes on the brink of tears.

Morbid curiosity encouraged me to take a peek at her. When I did, Birdy was only a few showerheads away from me, smirking while flaunting. She gave me the impression that she was truly relishing our time together, and no matter how poorly I reacted, she fully believed I was enjoying it as well.

Watching her against my better judgement, Birdy began to caress the shower knobs. "*You sure you don't want just a taste?*" She moaned, then cranked them both. Full pressure water shot down at her chest, and as if she were a slow-cooked slab of ribs, meat fell effortlessly from her bones. Seconds later there was pounds of ebony flesh heading towards the large drain, clogging it and allowing the blood to pool.

What remained of Birdy after she wash her chest and face was a skeletal figure with patches of torn flesh left hanging. When she turned her head towards me again, most of her skull was visible. Transfixed and gazing, I could see behind her eyeball and into the socket. Devoid of lips, only half her smiled shined now, but as she crept closer, it somehow widened.

In attempt to flee, I faked right and darted to my left. Then, before I knew it, I was in the air, my feet slightly above my head. When I came down, the back of my noggin was the first to make contact with the slippery floor. As soon as the knock came, I went black, and when I came to, I was back in my room.

So now my head KILLS, but at least I escaped. I just had to get that down on paper before I pass out again, which will surely be soon. My eyes lids are heavy but I think that might just be the head trauma talking. Getting knocked out came in clutch though, didn't it? I can't tell you if anyone else has ever been spared from rape by getting a concussion, but I can definitely say this is the most grateful headache I've ever had.

Okay, back to it.

The days that followed my run-in with the blonde were a bloated blur. I stayed inside all day Sunday, called in Monday and Tuesday, and did nothing with that time other than ponder endlessly in my living room, where I also had been sleeping. I didn't check my bedroom for the first day and a half. Sooner or later, I did manage to stomach it and open the door though.

My bed was disheveled but nothing more. There wasn't any blood, no pile of entrails or skin, only a messy bedroom. When I saw the lack of carnage it just supported the notion that I had lost my mind. Yet I felt relief seeing that all the blood had vanished. For a day or two, I even considered the idea that my experience was a one-time thing. A brief window of psychosis that rocked me to my core. Sort of like an intense acid flashback.

Midweek I returned to work with my head down. I was adamant on avoiding my boss especially, but also my coworkers and even customers when they were around. Luckily no one was suspicious of me though. Marge stayed up in her office, only making eye contact with me once, and my coworkers respected the distance I kept. But then again, I don't think any of them gave two shits if something was troubling me in the first place.

I wasn't very close to any of the dudes I worked with, yet they all knew the type of life I lived. They all had families, so they were occasionally in awe of how I spent my weekends, or the girls I reportedly slept with. I'd say they were envious because none of us were that far apart in age. Excluding Marge, all of us were in our mid-twenties to early-thirties. They just went a different route in life than me is all; a safer, more rewarding route, I'll admit. Therefore, if I came into work hungover or crabby from partying, it was the least of their concerns.

Be that as it may, I wasn't feeling ill that week at all—quite the opposite actually. I hadn't drunk or done any blow since the night of the living dead blonde. In fact, my plan immediately after was to detox, which I did. I drank boat loads of water, ate clean, and got as much sleep as I could afford. I even worked out that week (I sat in the sauna) to sweat out any toxins. By Thursday I was cleaner than a right winger's favorite handgun.

But I still thought of the blonde. How could I not? And not long after I started to ponder over the cashier as well. I wondered if that was a similar situation. Had she actually been scarred? Or was it my mind that had skinned that girl's face? I had no way to know, so I stayed guessing. I certainly wasn't going to tell a doctor about my experiences—not because I don't like them, but because it wasn't in my budget. I'd rather repress my insanity than die in crippling medical debt. I am American, after all. Going to the doctor is a Canadian luxury. Lucky bastards.

Considering the circumstances, I wish I could say I had planned to kick drugs completely then, but that's not how it went. I shortly tabled quitting, but I never committed. Which sounds RIDICULOUS when I think about it now. Like, at what point would I actually start to take care of myself? What was it going to take? If I hadn't been locked up, I'd probably still being doing them. And if I was really lucky, I'd be dead by now.

Early on, I had an easygoing weekend in mind. I envisioned myself relaxing in my living room—still wary of my bedroom—where I'd brainlessly watch TV and likely masturbate. Not to whatever was on the TV though. I'm just saying, in general, I'd jerk off. That reminds me: you know what's strange? Despite being deathly afraid of women, I still masturbate to the image of them. Isn't that weird?

ANYHOO, I digress. My lounging plans for the weekend were thrown to the side when my longtime friend, practically brother, Jordan called and reminded me of his trip up to the city. He told me he'd be in Chicago by Friday night with his wife and their small daughter. Or, as I used to know her as, my niece.

I wanted to flake but his visit was planned months in advance. They had already purchased plane tickets, booked a hotel, made special reservations; their whole fuckin' vacation was already on the move. They were in the city for—his wife— Shelby's birthday, and I damn well knew that. I couldn't bail now. Hell, it was even sort of my idea for them to come up! When Christie and I were dating, I spent weeks convincing Jordan to come down to Chicago for their next vacation, which landed on Shelby's birthday. So, in reality, convincing Jordan to come really meant convincing Jordan to convince Shelby.

It wasn't easy: he told me she wasn't initially thrilled on the idea of traveling with their toddler daughter. Not only the traveling portion, but she was also concerned with her daughter's behavior at certain attractions. Shelby personally wanted to see Chicago's great museums on art and history, and she feared that Kenzie would be unruly in the setting. Before she wound up accepting the trip, Shelby claimed that they'd regret going to Chicago the same day they arrived. (Call it women's intuition.)

Jordan persisted though. We hadn't seen each other since Kenzie was born, and while we both understood that life was different now, we missed each other. And at the time of convincing him, I wanted him to meet Christie. Back then I felt he *had* to meet her because I was sure she'd be around for the long haul. I can't speak for him—particularly after what happened—but out of all the people I've become acquainted with, Jordan was the only person I considered a true friend.

Our bond began in middle school. At thirteen we played in the same baseball league and ended up on the same team by chance. Through dozens of practices and games, our friendship grew, and post season, we still hung out often. After middle school, we tackled high school together, and at fifteen, we blended in with the stoners. Then came the parties, tons of girls, and experimenting with light drugs, which was all a blast. And our friendship flourished from every experience.

On top of being inseparable, we thrived together and encouraged self-improvement. I helped Jordan gain confidence, thus the ability to talk to girls, stand up for himself, and say what he actually means. In return he encouraged me not to limit myself, not to be so pessimistic, and most importantly, he kept me out of trouble.

Unfortunately, his good influence was short lived. I dropped out of high school our junior year, and he went to college the year after, just like he always planned. There he met Shelby and they got married about four years later. They stayed in Florida where Jordan secured a job with something to do with meteorology—I'm still not certain what that is, but apparently, it's not a weatherman like I thought. Then, three years later, they had a precious and healthy baby girl and named her Kenzie.

Early Saturday morning, Jordan informed me that they'd be heading to Millennium Park around lunch time. He said they were wanting to grab a bite to eat with me, and if I wanted, I could tag along to the art institute and the aquarium afterwards. Keeping my disinterest concealed, I said I'd love to and that I'd meet them at the Bean.

Now, to be truthful, I felt pretty good making my way to Millennium. I'd been clean for almost a full week and my head was the clearest it had been since could remember. Considering how joyous and p felt, I eventually started to warm up to the idea of a museum trip with Jordan and his family.

Approaching the park, I even started to get flat-out excited. Kenzie was just a newborn the last time I saw her, so I knew she didn't have a clue who I was, but that's what committed me to spending the day with them. I was determined that she remember me going forward.

I made it to Millennium before they had. Per usual there was a marginally large crowd around. Tourist were snapping photos in the Bean's reflection, parents were chasing their kids, and folks were chatting and laughing away. Aside for a few womanly eyes on me, everything seemed chill.

Standing out in the open so they could easily see me, my phone began to vibrate in my pocket. Jordan was calling.

"Yello?"

"We're close! Shelby and I are walking up with Kenzie leading the way. I think we see you."

I twirled around and tried to spot him. "Where you at? I don't see you."

"Oh, well, I think that's you we're staring at but I could be wrong. Here, why don't you scream really loud so we know it's you."

"Ha-ha, why can't I just wave?"

"So we can approach just anyone waving in the park? We'd be here all day. Brady, you have to scream, it's the only way. And do it like you're in *Dragonball Z*—Super Sayian that shit, bitch."

"No need. I see you now."

"Damnit. I really wanted to see everyone stare at you like a crackhead." He chuckled, then got onto his daughter in the same breath. "Hey! Kenzie, don't walk too far ahead. Slow down."

"She being wild?"

"Big time. She's more excited about being in Chicago than we are. Must be a Bear's fan."

From approximately forty feet I saw the trio approaching. Behind were Jordan and Shelby, lethargically walking after their energetic daughter. Jordan had gained some weight but still resembled the same kid I played little league baseball with. Shelby, on the other hand, looked much thinner—but of course she had. She had just had a baby the last time I'd seen her. On the way over to me and Chicago's shiny Bean, they waved and offered a genuine smile, but it was dwarfed in comparison to their daughter's.

Their little girl's gregarious grin was as contagious as it was adorable. Looking like a mini version of her mother, Kenzie had her darkening blonde hair in a bun and a similar tank top on as well. But while Kenzie's outfit matched her mother's, there were some subtle differences. Shelby's outfit was mature and very casual, and Kenzie's more related to her age. Instead of regular leggings as bottoms, Kenzie's turned into a flowing ballerina's tulle.

I smiled at her from a distance and waved eccentrically, doing my best clown. In response, Kenzie lit up, smiling even larger, and then took off towards me. She quickly gained distance between her and her sluggish parents. At first it appeared that Jordan was going to jog after her, but once he saw my energy towards Kenzie, he slowed.

And he judged it correctly, because I was happy about it. The only fear I had was that she would trip over her short legs on the way, but I should've been suspicious instead of concerned for her.

Why was she so excited? There's no possible way she could've remembered me. Kenzie couldn't even open her eyes whenever I had last seen her.

Nevertheless, when she reached me, I scooped her up gladly and lovingly. I held her up like a proud father, far above my head and to the greatest extent of my arms. Her feet swung and kicked excitedly in the air as she giggled. For a moment, it was like holding happiness in physical form. I had never felt so in place and perfectly at ease…

Then she slipped out of my hands and plummeted to the concrete.

Kenzie rightfully bawled on the ground after making impact. Jordan and Shelby made it just a second too late. Concerned with the condition of their little girl, they tended to her instantly as I stood above, dumbfounded and ashamed. I felt all the nearby eyes on me from onlookers, heard all the gasp and mutters. Trying to collect myself I started to bend over to help but before I had the chance, I caught sight of my hands.

Still in my grip were Kenzie's arms.

Not the entire limb, but the soft skin of both. Dripping and slick, they felt like a pair of soaked dish gloves in my hands. My stomach churned and my eyes bugged. I then shot my eyes to Kenzie and saw it was true. All the skin had been removed from her arms, only muscle and veins were shown as blood puddled around the toddler and her parents.

To no surprise, Jordan confronted me with max aggression.

"What did you do, Brady? How did that even happen?" he shouted in my face.

Still holding onto the skin that she slipped out of, I looked at him absentmindedly. He continued to shout, but it all came as muffled, incoherent noise as I shuddered.

"What?" I quietly muttered out of fear and confusion.

"What? What do you mean? Are you fucking on something? Jesus-fuck, Brady, you've actually turned into a junkie, haven't you? You better hope Kenzie is okay or I'm putting my foot up your ass."

"Jordan! That's enough. She's fine." Shelby cut in.

At the sound of her reassuring tone, my eyes returned to Kenzie and her mother. The toddler had quit wailing and now she only quivered with soft sobs. Her outfit, which was once a hot pink, had been colored a murky brown red by the ongoing blood soaking it. Even Shelby had been dampened from embracing her.

Ceasing his berating at my side, Jordan turned to his calm wife and took their daughter.

"Take her. It was just an accident. Brady didn't mean to drop her, she just wiggled free. There's hardly a scrape on her. She's fine, see. Check her yourself." Shelby soothed.

I know it sounds preposterous, but excluding Kenzie's dismembered arms, Shelby was right.

Kenzie was fine. She had even quit crying altogether when her dad took ahold of her. By the time he was drying her eyes, she already had them back on me, with the same giddy smile before I dropped her.

She only started to cry again once Jordan walked away with her.

This left Shelby and I standing by the Bean.

I turned towards her, saw the blood smeared on her cheek from Kenzie, and she said, "Don't worry. Jordan will get over it, trust me. He's just a little over protective. But I saw how she was wiggling in your arms all excited. It's not on you, Brady…" she snickered lightly and put a hand on my arm. "It's actually kind of her fault. She's just a little flirt like her mom. She can't help it."

VIII

One 'Xaney' day.

It goes without saying, but dropping Kenzie and seeing her flayed arms only made things worse. I left Millenium Park in a frenzy once Shelby placed a hand on my arm and squeezed—a longing look in her eyes adding layers to her touch. In my haste I didn't even bother saying anything to Jordan before I ditched. I fled quickly and tossed the slimy skin of his daughter's arms in a nearby wastebin on the way home. Jordan never contacted me again after that day, but that in itself told me everything I needed to know.

I spent the rest of that Saturday blind drunk, just trying to forget all the grisly sights I had seen recently. The bottle of Captain Morgan I purchased near my apartment didn't stand a fucking chance. I downed about half of it under five minutes, attempting to ignore everything. I hated what accepting what I had seen implied. Just considering that I had lost my mind made me regret every sane day I ever wasted. I thought of all the drugs I popped, snorted, and smoked, and wondered which of them did me in. But of course, I knew that it must've happened overtime though. Little by little, or brain cell by brain cell. If that's even how that works.

The next day I was too hungover to even endure the smell of liquor, let alone keep drinking. Yet I still needed something to dampen my mind. As an alternative, I bought some Xanax to snuff my memory further. Smithers surprisingly did me a solid and dropped the pills off at my apartment. Unlike him to do any favors, he told me that he was already in the area.

Less than a half hour after setting it up, Smithers called me when he was near my place.

I answered with a low and sickly tone. "Hello?"

"Aye, yo, I'm outside, I think. Gotta find a spot to park the whip then I'm headed up."

"Sounds good, bro, but you should know that I'm super hungover. Feel pretty sick."

"You good. We'll be in and out."

Concealing my concern, I kept my voice calm and unsuspecting. "Who's *we*? Just curious."

"Me and my girl. See you in a sec. Third floor, right? You said F-three?"

"Y-yeah. Yessir. That's the apartment. Let me kno-" He hung up on me.

It wasn't until then when I first realized that, through my horrible recent experiences, I'd begun to fear a woman's presence. The way the peeled cashier and Shelby had looked at me was already embedded in my brain, but it was thoroughly recalled when I learned Smithers was bringing a woman up. With both Shelby and the cashier there was this gleam in their eyes that seemed familiar, yet hazardous; as if it were underlying with aggression or passion. It reminded me of how an old creep sitting at the bar stares at all the young women having fun, but also similar to the way a cat stares at a squirrel outside the window. Totally immersed and their wheels turning.

In addition to my revelation around women, I also gathered that I hadn't had an issue with men as far as blood and guts went. It was only women taking a 'special' interest in me, and it was only them who had shed their skin.

Soon after the call ended, a knock came at my door. I rushed over, eager for them to leave already. Before opening it, I was committed to paying Smither's lady friend no mind. I didn't know her and she didn't know me, which is the way I aimed to keep it.

But the second I opened my front door, a pair of leering dark eyes found me. To the left of Smithers was a Mexican woman, probably younger than twenty-five and no taller than five-three. One of the things that stood out about her—aside from her dark features and unsettling gaze—was her lengthy acrylic nails.

"Sup, bruh. Let us squeeze by ya real quick so we can do business."

Avoiding her eyes, I glued my focus to Smithers. "No! Wait, I mean, that's not a good idea. I-I just had an accident."

"Accident? Whatchu mean?"

Although I regretted the direction I took my excuse, I leaned into it. "You know…like on the floor…It just slipped out."

"Oh…word?" He grimaced; his girl stared. "Well, here's your shit then."

I gave him the dough quicker than he could take out the bottle of Xans. We swapped and I meant to close the door without a second look out. Though that's not what occurred. Shutting the door, I took one last glance at Smither's Latina lover.

Her eyes were still fixed on me, but more importantly, she was standing in a mess of her own blood. It was dripping from her torn open palms, down her legs, and to the floor. When Smither's was turning to leave, she didn't leave right away. She stayed still and kept digging into her palms with her long colorful nails.

If abused, Xanax can easily put someone in an extremely hazy place mentally. It's almost like a fugue state of mind. I've come to notice this more than once, as I've blacked out on Xanax almost every time that I've taken it. And if I didn't, then I didn't take enough.

Luckily (at least at first) I had bought an adequate amount and probably like twenty-five minutes after I took them, I was as dim as a dying bulb. I'm sure that I roamed around, snacked a little, and watched some TV, but I have no recollection of any of that. As far as I'm concerned, I was asleep for eleven hours. I wanted to forget; to not be conscious of what was happening, and Xanax made that happen for me.

Though forgetting was just temporary. Upon waking up, I discovered that my problem was inescapable.

I was in my bed when I came to, but far from comfortable. My arms had lost feeling as they were tied above my head and to my bed post. My legs were in a similar predicament. My vision was blurry with boogers of sleet in the corners and I fought to rub them clean, not yet comprehending the situation. When it dawned on me that being tied up was a bit unusual, I did everything in my power to get loose, but to no avail. The knots at the corners of my bed frame were eagle-scout tight.

Before I could even guess or accuse the culprit, she appeared at my bedroom door, dressed in leather lingerie and colored by candle light. Adriana leaned against the door frame, relaxed and staring at me on the bed. I had already begun to sweat and my stomach shrunk while she eyed me.

"Adriana? What the hell is going on?" I tried to pull myself free. "How did you even get in?"

Calmly, she said. "Door was unlocked. Figured you could use the company."

"To be honest, I think I can go without it. Why would you assume that?" I replied, keeping my voice casual but still trying to free myself.

"Heard about your ex."

"Oh…yeah." I halted my struggling briefly. "Shocked the hell out of me when I found out."

"Do you feel like it's your fault?"

"Huh?"

"I said, do you miss her at all?"

"That's not what you said. What'd you actually say?"

"So why haven't you called?" She threw another curveball.

"You?"

"Yes, me? Who the fuck else would I be asking for? I've been waiting." She spiked her tone and took two wrathful steps towards me.

Anxious about her intentions, I attempted to talk her down. "No, yeah, you're right. I'm sorry. I'm a dick, I know. I knew you were waiting. I've just been sick is all."

The aggression in her voice faltered. "Awh, but you've always been sick, Brady. In the head, I mean. You're my sick little puppy, aren't you?"

Back to pulling and twirling my wrist to get loose, Adriana came even closer.

For a moment she stood and looked at every corner of the bed, seemingly taking in her handy work. "Are the restraints tight enough? I don't want you moving too much."

"Can't we just talk, Aide? I'm not really in the mood and I do-"

She suddenly chuckled loudly, genuinely humored by what I said. "Aide? Since when do we do nicknames? Wait a minute, are you sweet talkin me because you're scared? You are, aren't you! That's too freaking cute."

I swallowed. "What are you going to do?" the panic in my voice becoming evident.

"Well, what do you want me to do?"

"Let me go."

Circling the bed slowly, she giggled. "Hm, I don't know about that. Certainly doesn't sound fun." she said, then laid a finger on my shin and slid it all the way up to my nipple. A trail of blood traced her path.

"Please, can we do this another time? You don't understand. I've been going through something. I really am sick."

"Oh, is that why you've been doing blow and popping Xans?"

I was nonplussed. The simple fact that Adriana caught me red-handed in a lie boosted my fear.

"There's still some coke on the counter out there. And as for the Xanax, I just guessed. I mean, how else could I have tied you to the bed without you waking up? You didn't stir a bit."

"All right, I'm not *that* sick, but I'm telling you, this isn't a good idea."

Swiftly Adriana bent over and scooped something off the floor then threw it on my chest. It was the blonde's G-string that she must've left behind in her fury.

"That was last week and it was a BIG mistake, trust me. I can even tell you about it, but I'll sound crazy." I pleaded, my words involuntarily speeding.

She nodded as if she understood, then sat on the bed next to my legs. After a troublesome grin appeared across her face, she put her hand on my crotch. Admittedly, I was hard, but simply from the fact that I had just woken up.

"If you're not wanting to fuck me, then what's this?" she gingerly cupped my package.

"Oh, come on. You know that's just morning wood."

"It's eleven-thirty at night."

"You know what I mean!" I shouted; my composure shattered. "Goddamn it! You stupid whore! Just let me go or I swear to God!"

The hostility in my voice brought forth her biggest smile yet.

She had left my boxers on the entire time, despite how vulnerable I had been. But that changed when she retrieved a pair of scissors from her purse.

"You don't care if I cut these do you?"

"Yeah, actually I do."

"YeAh AcTuAlLy I dO. Shut up." she mocked, then proceeded to cut up to the waistband of my underwear. The cold thin blade made me want to recoil, but I didn't have the room to do so. I only whimpered and tightly shut my eyes until they were off.

She carelessly tossed my underwear to the side and I watched them fall to the floor, accepting that I was now completely nude and entirely at her will.

Adriana continued by putting my softening erection in her mouth, and shockingly, I enjoyed it. My stiffness returned and I even started to moan while she swallowed me.

But any ecstasy I was riding was obliviated after she looked up at me.

Her lips were ripped clean off, but they could still be found midway down my shaft. Not only that but a half dozen of her teeth had also fallen out and landed in my pubic hair. While our eyes corresponded, blood poured from her mouth and within a minute, we were both drenched.

Ignoring my pleas, she slid off her leather panties and straddled me.

"Adriana, seriously, I'm begging! I can't take this." I whined, repressing my gagging. "Let me explain it to you, please."

"Awh, my little whiny boy." She smiled down at me, partly toothless. "*Cry about it*."

She then inserted myself inside her and began to ride me. Everything felt normal for all of thirty seconds, and then the fluids spewed. Blood and urine splashed in my eyes and mouth as she fucked herself harshly, chunks of her wet flesh fell between my legs, and once she leaned back, and her stomach split open, her innards stacked on top of my gut.

Fading swiftly with an upset stomach and a featherlight head, I saw that she had grinded her bottom half down to her pelvic bone. The meat and tissue of her thighs, butt, and vagina were turned into a fleshy mush and spread across the mattress. And from feeling herself sensually, she warped any raw beauty she had once possessed. Before I eventually fainted, her face resembled a crude bust sculpted by a careless child while she rode me.

IX

Self-diagnoses. A sign.

I clearly had bigger problems, so I didn't bother returning to work. You might be wondering what I intended to do about bills and other expenses, but truth is, I didn't have a plan. That would've been too wise; which I am not. And additionally, it's pretty easy to not care about such things when you're on a bender; which I was. I didn't stop taking Xanax after Adriana's ambush. In the state of mind I'd been isolated by, I needed it more than ever. But I also needed to make sure I locked my fucking front door this time, too. Just as long as I did that, I'd be fine. Or so I hoped.

About midweek I hit up Smithers for more pills and he told me to pull through within an hour. As you know, we weren't the best of friends, so anytime I came to his house it was pleasantly brief. He never asked too many questions, never expected me to hang out, and on the best days, he'd even meet me in his driveway.

Though unfortunately for me, Smithers must've had a change of heart regarding our 'friendship'. Or maybe he was merely suspicious of me and the way I behaved when him and his girl dropped off the pills. Can't be too sure. I'm only guessing here, but the way our conversation went when I popped over definitely supported that hunch.

Sitting in his driveway, I sent him a text to let him know I was outside. And the amount of sheer disappointment I felt when he responded was gigantic. He told me to come inside.

When I first got ahold of him about buying, the possibility of running into his girlfriend again made me incredibly anxious. I held out hope though and believed it would be as quick and easy as any other time. I thought, if I was lucky enough, he'd run outside, grab the bones, throw me the pills and that'd be the end of it. Just as easy as one, two, three.

But more often than not, the best-case scenario is also the least likely.

Reluctantly I left my car and headed up Smither's steps leading to his door. I knocked with rhythm, the least of cop-like ways, and instead of answering, he shouted. "Come in! It's unlocked!" Preparing to see the worst, I took a deep breath and lightly slapped my own face before opening the door.

"Aye, man." He threw up a backwards peace sign, the TV's program illuminating his face.

"Hey." I nodded in a 'Sup' fashion.

Smithers was sitting on the couch, leaned forward and rolling a blunt. Just smithers. No girlfriend in sight. On the coffee table near his grinder and bong were the bottle of Xanax I came for. Upon seeing it, my money started to burn a hole through my pocket. I took out the cash and laid it on the table.

"Here's the sixty, man. Is the whole bottle me?"

"Yep. That's all you, but pop a squat for me."

My face warmed. "Do what?"

"Sit your ass down. Chill for a sec, bruh. Tryin' not to have people in and out of the house. Think my neighbors gettin suspicious." He licked the seal of his wrap. "You smoke?"

Finding a spot to squat, I landed in a chair diagonal from him. Right at the start my hands were already so clammy that I had to wipe them off on my sweat pants as I sat. The recliner I chose was beat to shit and partly burned with cigarettes, but the biggest piece of damage was the fabric and cushion that had been torn off the right arm. Instead of responding to Smither's question, I gazed at the hard plastic of the chair's body. In that moment, I couldn't help but think I was looking at the bones of the furniture.

"Aye, yo. Answer." Smithers snapped. "Do.you.smoke?"

"Huh? Oh, no. Sorry. I'm just a little tired. I don't smoke, not anymore. I used to when I was a teenager."

"Oh yeah? what happened? Too good for the ganj now?"

"Nah, that's not it. Weed just makes me paranoid is all." I said, and a subtle noise in another room followed. I shot up to my feet, alarmed. "What was that? Is your girl here?"

Smithers peered at me, taken back by my frantic and sudden gesture. "What? She ain't here. I already kicked that bitch to the curb, for real. It wasn't going to work out. Just sit down, you're freaking me out and I'm trying to smoke this blunt."

I returned to my seat, fairly embarrassed. "My bad. Sorry about that."

"Yeah, you said that, but why are you so interested in Gabby?"

"Who?"

"Gabby. My ex? You just asked if she were here. How do you know her?"

"I don't. The other day was the very first time I'd ever seen her."

"*Bruh*, that's cap. You were sweatin' bullets when we showed up at your place. Nervous as hell. Did you hit or somethin'?"

"No, I really didn't. I don't know her, I swear." I hastily defended.

"Chill. I ain't got any beef. I told you that I got rid of her, didn't I?"

"But I honestly never had sex with her. I didn't even know her name until you told me."

"Then why did you ask?"

"Ask what?"

"If she were here, dumbass. Goddamn, bro, are you tweaking? What's your deal?"

Suddenly I was considering telling him everything. There was a part of me that suggested he'd listen, and I searched for any reason why he would. I never knew much about Smithers, but he always struck me as a guy who'd seen some serious shit in his time. But I knew it wasn't like anything I'd seen lately, or he'd be worse off. Nevertheless, I was vulnerable and I needed a friend; or just an ear to bend.

"I think I'm losing my mind." I said, packaged with conviction.

"Stressed out?" he replied, lighting the thin opening of his blunt.

"Yeah, you could say that, but it's more than just stress…I'm seeing things."

Smithers straightened his laxed posture on the couch, his interest piqued. "Whatchu mean by that? Like in your head?"

"I'm not sure…sometimes I think it's not just in my head."

"Wait a minute, are you a schizo? That shit is next level crazy. What are you seeing?"

It was the first chance I had to convey it, but as warm as I initially was to the idea of telling him, I found myself struggling to explain. Around then all I knew was women—all women; even little girls—had become smitten with me, but their skin was as malleable as a stick of butter, and flesh stripped from their bodies just as easy as peeling an orange. But how do I explain it on the spot and to someone like Smithers?

"It's kind of hard to put into wo-"

"Yo, this one time I saw this video of a dude walking his dog and this motherfucker just stopped and started talking like he'd just ran into someone. Even the dog looked confused. A lil' of me thought he was just faking for views, but I looked it up later. They really do see shit like that."

"That's wild, but that doesn't really sound like the type of stuff I'm seeing."

"Oh, word? What is it then?" He took a drag, coughed then chuckled. "*Dead people?*"

I hesitated at first, but went ahead and spilled it. "They're not dead, but they look like it."

That shut up Smithers quick. He could only look at me while the blunt burned in his hand. I think he was processing what I had said and was trying to find out if I was pulling his leg.

"What exactly are you seeing?" he asked, sincerity in his tone.

"It's just… women. But it's women that I actually know or the ones right in front of me. It's the ones talking to me or looking at me from across the room."

"I don't understand. If they're actually there, then why are you so scared that you see them?"

"They're not the same though. They all try to touch me and thei-"

"That doesn't sound awful." He smirked.

To prevent further interruptions from Smithers, I spit out my uncensored perception around my dilemma. "It's like they're all aggressively flirting with me, but they get a kick out of mutilating themselves when I'm around. Seriously, it's like something out of *Saw*. I've seen women rip their stomachs open and have their guts spill out. Some of them misshape their faces and end up looking deformed but they still pursue me. … I realize how this sounds, but I promise it's true… I- I think I must've fried my brain or something like it."

Smithers tapped the ash of his soon-to-be roach and hit it once more. "That's pretty fucked up, man." he said flatly, seeming unmoved.

I shook my head forlornly. "Right…"

"Did you go see a doctor about it?"

"No. I don't want to."

Smithers coughed harshly, a small laugh following. "Yo, what? Ha-ha, you crazy as fuck, boy."

"That's what I'm trying to tell you."

"So, if you're not planning to go see a doctor, then what's your plan? You just gonna sweat it out? Meditate or some bullshit?"

"I'm not sure. I guess I was thinking of locking myself in my apartment and finding a job I could do from home." That was a lie. I hadn't thought of that at all.

"You'd still have to go outside sometime. And from the way you put it, it sounds like these freaky women would find you anyway."

"Yeah, you're probably right."

"On God."

"Yeah."

He smashed out what was left of his blunt and fetched a cigarette from his pack. "What did Gabby do to freak you out so bad? Because in reality, that bitch was on her phone the entire time we were over at your place."

"She was just starring at me, but she had torn her palms open with her nails and was standing in a puddle of her blood."

"Damn… And you're not fucking with me?"

"I wish I was."

Even though expressing my outrageous troubles to someone had felt good, it didn't exactly improve anything. I was still relatively doomed. And plus, I'm not even sure Smithers believed me. He seemed fairly chill about the whole ordeal, but that's likely because it wasn't happening to him.

"Well, my guy." he stretched his arms above his head and groaned. "I guess I can ask my plug if he can get some schizo meds for my next pick up. Get it for you pretty cheap, too. I bet he'll have some already. They even have some pills that make your sack stop growing hair, if that interest you."

I stood from the beaten chair, implying my departure. "Thanks, man, but I'm just going to hope it's not something like schizophrenia."

"Ha-ha, whatchu mean? The fuck else it gonna be? You got beef with a witchdoctor? Been playing around with voodoo? Of course it's something mental! There's no other option."

I can't tell you why his attempt at humor regarding my troubles struck me like it had, but nevertheless, I actually pondered over what he said.

All of a sudden, I was thinking in different terms than before. I started to consider the supernatural; an angle in which I'd never even glanced at. Wrapping my head around it, I started to pace in Smithers' living room.

"Do you think that's a possibility?"

"Is what a possibility?"

"Like do you think it could be something like that? Like a curse?"

"No? That shit's dumb. Of course you're not cursed. No one is. If any of that stuff was real, men would be walking around with curses all over them. How would you even stop them from cursing people in the first place?"

"Them." I muttered. "Do you think that witchcraft is really out there?"

"Didn't I just tell you no?"

"Oh, yeah. Sorry about that. Just forget it." I apologized, but hadn't mentally dropped the subject.

"I bet they're just weird acid flashbacks or whatever. Or maybe your brain really is dying. Who knows."

"Not me." I shrugged, but soon I was determined to find out.

Whether he meant to or not, Smithers inspired me to get to the bottom of it. I was leaning towards it being something mental, like he suggested, but the idea of a hypothetical curse was still humoring me— in a completely unfunny way.

Before leaving Smithers', I asked him if he still had some blow. He confirmed that he did without even checking and I bought about a gram from him on top of my Xanax. Forking over the coke, he warned me not to speedball with them, but sold them both to me anyway.

That night I put the pills aside and only stuck to the yayo. For what I intended to do all weekend, uppers were the way to go. I spent twenty hours reading articles and skimming blogs about hallucinations as well as any mental illness comparable to what I was experiencing.

You can imagine my feelings when I didn't find jack shit in my medical search. Not a single form of psychosis matched the conditions I now had to live with. The only help offered was psychiatric treatment via ad, which was just an online survey. Once I answered all the questions, they hid the results and asked me to rate their website. (Three stars.)

Eventually, as a last resort, I started to look into witchcraft, voodoo, and the occult. Somehow there was even more articles on these subjects than anything else I was researching. But each articles contrasted and contradicted the one that came before and after it. It was as if sociologists couldn't land on the same page with any of their findings. I could hardly find anything that was crystal clear; most if it were stories of ancient or secret civilizations, bizarre rituals, or vivid paintings of crowds dancing around fires.

I had almost given up, but then I saw it. On a website called 'thedevilsdue.com', there was a whole category of curses from cults and covens alike. Upon digging, I thought that more than half of the reports were fictional, but I guess if I told someone about my foul experiences—besides Smithers—they'd think I was lying, too. Speaking of which, do *you* even believe me?

Wait, never mind. I don't want to know. Let's just keep going.

In this dark and questionable corner of the web, I stumbled upon what was essentially a catalog of unnamed emblems. About all of the symbols were framed in circles; sometimes it'd be a goat in the center, other times a tree, the moon, or even just a grand fire. But the one that stuck out to me was perhaps the most ambiguous.

Its relevance hit me like a stiff slap to the back of the head. The black rim, its slim tall center and the hallow spaces near the edge; it was agonizingly familiar. I knew where I'd seen the symbol within a minute of having my eyes glued to it.

It was the same symbol hanging in Grandma Debra's house.

X

The confrontation.

When I finally went to bed after obsessively researching for nearly twenty-four hours, I only had one thing on my mind. The obscure symbol I saw online and formally at Debra's house was now tattooed on all my thoughts. I tried my hardest to stay grounded about it, but my drug-induced imagination made matters difficult. I didn't know what or how to think.

Do I immediately assume that Debra practiced witchcraft and in the spirit of vengeance for her granddaughter, she put a hex on me? Yeah, you bet your ass that's what I assumed! And by the end of the night, I was pretty damn certain of it. But I wasn't in the right frame of mind; I was exhausted, and even then, I gathered that the entire concept was flat-out ridiculous.

My plan was to sleep on it for a few days and see what I thought then. If the idea still seemed real, then I'd do something about it. I didn't know *what* exactly by that point, but by-God, I was going to do it.

Three days later I felt no different.

The scenario of a curse hadn't left my concerns in the slightest. It didn't help that I spent a lot of that time staring at the emblem on my phone though. I woke up with it, ate my meals with it, and basically went to bed with it every night. In a way the photo of the symbol became a new obsession all by itself. When I looked at it, not only was I trying to guess its roots, it also strangely brought me to think of

Christie. And that train of thought led me to feel like I deserved what was happening, as if I had boughten the curse firsthand, and the emblem was proof of purchase.

On the third day, I made a plan to do some deep investigating. I knew showing up at Debra's house wasn't going to be well received. There isn't a contradiction or a 'but' with that either. She was bound to be furious or just downright horrified that she even saw my face, let alone me knocking on her door to see if she had deliberately ruined my life. However, even if she were welcoming about my visit, that would be reason for concern as well.

A part of me feared that she'd react to me the same way all the other women had, but for some inexplainable reason, I figured that wouldn't be the case. It was just an inkling I had. You know that rushing feeling you get when your close to solving something and the closer you get, instinct just takes over?

Yeah? Well, that doesn't happen to me, so I anticipated being wrong and was scared shitless.

I couldn't recall precisely where she lived, but I knew the general area. It was a clean and fairly charming neighborhood complimented by several houses built from either brick or stone. Not a total suburb, but similar. As far as I had seen the only type of residents they had were families and presumably other grandparents. The street appeared freshly paved, the sidewalks clear, and the trees along the road were regularly trimmed, but not rendered shadeless.

If it weren't for me remembering her last name, I don't know if I ever would have found her house. I just happened to see 'PETERSON' in blocky letters on the mailbox and it clicked for me. I almost threw myself at my windshield from how sudden I hit my brakes, but once I was at a stop, I reversed and parked on the street right out front.

It was a little past five-thirty when I arrived, but I didn't leave the car until after seven. I had to build up the courage to knock on her door, as well as find out what I was going to say. Therefore, I sat in my car and did key bumps for over an hour, trying to find the best tactic to approach with. But I soon realized that there was no correct way to go at it. Each explanation I came up with seemed faulty and I knew she'd see right through it.

No reasoning I came up with sounded better than the truth. I might as well have walked up her deck steps, knocked, then said, *Hey, Debra! Remember me? Christie's ex-boyfriend? The one that got her hooked on the drugs which ultimately killed her? Oh, you do remember! Great! Can I come in?* Or how about, *Debra! You ole' bitch, you! How the hell are ya? Would you mind if I squeezed by you and checked your cluttered house for any signs of witchcraft?*

Eventually I said fuck it and left the car and hurried up to her door, ignoring any negative thoughts or outcomes. I knocked twice, and vaguely anticipated the door to open and then slam back in my face, but there was no answer.

So, I knocked again.

Nothing.

Knowing that I shouldn't but doing it anyway, I took a peek through the glass panel on the door. I didn't see anyone. It was just the same unorganized and dusty house I spent thanksgiving at. Though while I tried to catch a glimpse inside, I heard muffled music playing. That encouraged me to think that she was home, but hadn't heard my knocking.

So, I rapped on the door even harder. Four times to be exact.

No response came. The thin curtains nearby didn't even stir. Allowing my stupidity to fully take over, I tried the door knob. But of course, it was locked.

Disappointed but not yet discouraged, I stepped back from the door and took a gander around the house. With the sun setting I could see a small window with lights on inside. I believed it to be the kitchen, but it was too high up for me to check.

Trying my luck, I went around the house and through her chain linked fence. Despite that it was the time of year to acknowledge sprouting flowers and fruitful crops, every plant in her garden was shriveled and black. And near the beds of dead flowers was a decently sized porch, but the modest size of the property made the porch appear jarringly large.

At the top of the steps there was a sliding glass door with red curtains hiding the inside. I stared at the door from the base of the steps, deciding if it were actually necessary for me to be there. Consequences like her calling the police and them finding drugs on my person or in my vehicle crossed my mind, and so did lawfully getting shot. It wasn't typical for an elderly woman to have a gun handy, but then again, nothing about my life had been very typical as of late.

But as it turns out, there wasn't a chance in hell I could've predicted the outcome anyway. Nothing could have prepared me for Debra's reaction. It's seared into my memory just as vividly as that kid losing his ear and eye on the fourth of July, or any of the gruesome women that followed years later.

I snorted and swallowed any drip in the back of my throat the coke had left, then quickly scaled the steps. A dim motion sensory light flicked on when I made it to the top; its bulb perhaps days away from burning out completely. I place my hand on the door's handle, not even considering that it could be locked as well, and pulled slowly. The door slid back without much force, and the smell of freshly cooked pasta approached me once I walked past the curtain.

Fleetwood Mac was giving her dinner a soundtrack. I could tell that the sounds and smells were coming from directly ahead of me, past three closed doors and across the living room. I proceeded with caution, wondering if I should retreat before I was in too deep. Given that I had already broken in and was blitzed on blow, I knew the chances of it going smoothly were steep, but I was too desperate to back out. And whilst creeping in Debra's halls, I became even more confident that she was the cause of my condition.

I passed the living room and stopped at the corner of the kitchen, just out of Debra's sight. She was at the island counter, slicing tomatoes and humming with the sounds of the seventies. All in all, she looked peaceful. Watching her, I was aware it was my last chance to ditch, but regretfully, I declined.

I stepped into the kitchen and softly knocked on the wall I just crossed.

She jolted and flung around to face me; her eyes enflamed with surprise. She then gasped and got in a defensive stance, backing up around the counter. Right from the get-go trouble was found.

Our gazes were tied across the counter, but suddenly her eyes fell from mine. I followed where hers went and it didn't take a genius to know what she was staring at. A phone lay in the middle.

"I know what you're thinking, but please, just hold on a se-"

Debra practically threw herself at it, and I did the same. She managed to grab it first, but I grabbed her hands and tried to take it away. While she yelped and struggled, she fought to dial 911. And I hung up when I was able to wrestle it away from her.

After tossing the phone, I looked to deescalate things. I put my hands up while I spoke. "Please, don't panic. I'm not here to hurt you, I swear. It's okay. I knocked on the door a couple of times but there was no answer."

"So, you just came in through the back? What the hell is the matter with you? Stay away from me!" she hissed, then added space between us by backing around the counter again. Fluently she swiped the knife off the counter and pointed it at me.

"You really don't have to worry, I told you I wasn't going to hurt you and I meant that. I'm not here for anything bad. I'll stay over here and you stay over there, fine by me. Just please relax." I pleaded, my hands surrendering to the point of the blade. "Do you remember me?"

She worriedly shook her head. "No! Who the hell are you and why are you in my house?"

I was taken back, and partly feeling as if I made a mistake already. "You really don't remember me? I'm Christie's old boyfriend. We spent Thanksgiving together last year, remember? You made this Oreo pie for her and we all ate it at the kitchen table over there." I nodded towards the round table near us.

"Christie's dead!"

My face couldn't help but squish in confusion. "I know that? Trust me, I know. I only came he-"

"She was in her bed when I found her, you know…Stiff as a board and her nose leaking blood and her mouth foaming…" Suddenly her bottom lip trembled and her gaze lost its focus from me. "My precious Chrissy, gone just like her mother."

Hearing the intricacies of the scene pierced me. "I'm so sorry you had to see her like that, Debra…I'm sorry it even came to that. You have no idea what I would do to go back and help her. I know she meant the world to you, and she was crazy about you, too."

"You knew her?" she asked incredulously, the hand holding the knife went limp as she seemed genuinely confounded.

I had seen the same look of lost in my father's eyes before he got real sick. While I was glad that she was losing interest in stabbing me, I was worried she'd grown senile in recent months. It had never occurred to me that, with Christie's death, her grandmother had declined mentally.

"Yes, ma'am. My name is Brady, I was her boyfriend."

"And you say that you loved her?"

"More than anything."

In response she groaned and stumbled as if she were lightheaded and close to fainting. To stabilize herself, Debra reached out with her free hand and leaned on the counter. The knife still lazily in her other hand.

"Are you okay?" I dared to take a step closer to her.

She stopped me by stiffening her knife hand and aiming it at my chest. "Don't come any closer...I'm fine... I just get a little mixed up these days. What did you say your name was?"

For the first time since she spotted me, I put my hands down to my side. "My name is Brady. Christie and I had started dating more than a year ago...and if I'm being honest, I had never loved someone so much. She was perfect, and temporarily improved my life by making it worth living."

Debra took a moment to reply. "That does sound like my Chrissy." She smirked, tears sitting on her eye lids in remembrance.

"Yeah, she was the best. Hands down the sweetest and funniest person I've ever met... she also impressed everyone who laid eyes on her. It's hard for me to believe that she even wanted anything to do with me…"

"Sounds like you really cared about her." she said, her smile still thinly there.

"I did."

At first, I thought she started to sob after failing to hold it in. Her eyes shut and she turned away from me. But what I had originally thought were whimpers, turned out to be giggles. Once she turned back to me, she was full on cackling. Out of discomfort, I laughed with her. I guess I just figured we were laughing off the tension, but when she ceased her chuckling, I realized it had been an inside joke.

"So, if you really cared about her, then why did you do what you did?"

I felt as if she had just taken the knife to my gut. I couldn't fathom what I had heard through her clenched teeth.

"What's that?"

Her grip tightened around the knife's handle. "You gullible, disgusting little pig… I know who you are, Brady Morgan. I know what you did, and I know why you're here."

My heart, which was already in the pit of my stomach, dropped even further. "You know why I'm here?"

Her smile reappeared, but with a sinister touch. The corners of her mouth stretched higher than I could've predicted and most of her teeth were shown. With her grin so immense, her skin was taut and reached a point where her face appeared mask-like. I froze in anticipation as she stared at me.

"I was beginning to think you'd never show." she said, a wisp of pleasure present.

And then she stabbed herself.

The blade went deep into her neck, just below her jaw. Blood coated her hand instantly, but once she dragged the knife across her throat, it spewed.

"NO!" I dove to reach her.

I caught her before she slumped to the floor, but in doing so, covered myself in her fast-flowing blood. I put my hand over her gaping neck and applied pressure—just what I'd seen in movies—but it was no use. The wound was too wide. Almost as wide as the smile she still held.

"Why did you do that?" I shrieked. "I need your help!"

Convulsing in my arms while her feet kicked wildly on the kitchen floor, Debra yanked me closer by the collar of my shirt. With her dying breath, she whispered. "D-D-Don't for-forget y-your jacket."

Mystified, I begged her to repeat what she had said, but it was too late. Debra was dead, yet remained leering at me with still green eyes and a frozen grin below.

XI

Dried Blood. Mother of Three.

Before Debra lay dead at my fcet, I had never seen a corpse in person. I know what you're thinking: *But what about the women who dismembered themselves, Brady?* I've literally splashed in blood and seen more vital organs than Charles Manson, so I understand questioning the sentiment. But the thing is, those women weren't really dead, were they? Corpses don't have agendas. And they sure as hell don't talk dirty and try to fuck you either.

A puddle of blood almost the size of the kitchen began to dry minutes after she died. To me, it was just another clear indication of how real it was. Before, I had never seen such a large amount of blood clot, but now coagulated blood stained the linoleum, as well as my clothes and my bare arms along with part of my chin.

For the first ten minutes I sat on her island counter and did nothing but stare and try to make sense of what occurred. My eyes didn't leave her dead body, as if I was entranced by it. Whenever I finally stepped to it, I felt I had gazed into Debra's eyes just as long as I used to stare into Christie's. The resemblance really was uncanny; the woman shared Christie's looks as if she were her own mother instead of a grandparent.

I even felt obliged to touch her face while I was there. Not in a sick and twisted way though. I just felt her flesh to see if it caved or came off like it had with other women, and it didn't. Her flesh was cold, but stayed intact. Touching her boney cheeks and arms, it dawned on me that it had been the first time in a while that I'd been able to touch a woman and not have her look like roadkill afterwards… Only catch was that she was already dead. Ironic, isn't it?

Now, I'm not a complete idiot. I was aware that Debra's wasn't the best place to be at the moment. It didn't take a master criminal to know that there was a chance the police were on their way, following up on the call. Even if it was just a misdial, it's better to be safe than sorry. Or that'd be my approach if I was a cop anyway. And in this particular case, I'd be right to check in. Which is why I needed to get the hell out of there pronto.

But Debra's last words still rung in my ears. I hadn't figured out what she meant. What was it supposed to mean: 'Don't forget your jacket.' I didn't even wear a jacket over. Had she realized what she was saying? Or had I misheard her?

I wasn't comfortable accepting that possibility. I felt I had heard her correctly. She said, 'Don't forget your jacket', as if she were a mother forewarning her child of the cold before setting out to play.

But why?

Why did she tell me not to forget my jacket?

What jacket?

I asked myself these questions several times in the wake of her suicide, yet I was eager to leave. The mental image of flashing red and blue lights appearing outside Debra's windows put fear in my heart. I was almost confident they were on their way the longer I stayed, but I still wanted to investigate. I knew I'd never be in Debra's house again.

I hopped off the counter and stepped over her body. Then I hurried to the living room and surveyed the space from the middle. The black symbol in which inspired my visit stared back at me, almost taunting me with its mystique. At that moment I wanted nothing more than to chuck it through the window, but I resisted. Instead, I moved things around and looked for anything that seemed remotely helpful. Though I didn't really know what 'helpful' consisted of. I think by this point I was beginning to see how truly helpless I was.

I carried into the hallway and tried to decide which door to check first. One was a bathroom, while the other two were surely bedrooms. I knew for a fact one of them was Christie's old room since she had taken me on a little tour of the house last time. Really all that was on the other side of her door were movie posters from the early 2000s, old clothes in the closet, and her bed. With that in mind, I skipped it. And on top of that, I also didn't want to visit Christie's death site.

That decision left me with only one choice. I approached the door that wasn't Christie's or the bathroom and barged in. Upon stepping inside, I told myself I'd only stay for no more than four minutes longer.

The room would've been pitch black had it not been for a slim desk lamp in the corner. Considering the clear drawers at the left of the desk, I assumed it to be a crafts table the light sat on. I looked inside the drawers briefly, but all I saw were beads, powders, and used notebooks. None of it seemed valuable to my cause.

The rest of the room was mostly taken up by Debra's bed and dresser, but that held my attention only fleetingly. My focus reunited with the desk with the lamp, or more particularly, what the light was directly shining on. The black jacket I had worn last Thanksgiving was folded on top of the table; the lamp rigged to work as a spotlight for it. The presentation reminded me of *Raiders of the Lost Ark*, but I was far from feeling like Indy.

I gawked down at my jacket before I reached for it. As soon as I had my hands on it and the folds came undone, a plain envelope fell out. There was no stamp, no address, and it wasn't even sealed. It just had '*Brady*' written in the center.

Hurriedly I snatched the envelope from the carpeted floor and took out its contents. Inside was a letter, more than half of the page filled out. As I remember, it said:

> *Brady,*
> *If you're reading this then I'm certain it is because you have come to my house in desperation and in search for answers. It's no secret to me that you have been living in great peril lately, but you must know that I don't pity you. Nor do I believe that anyone else should pity you. When we first met, I promptly gathered that you were bad for Christie, but I didn't know the full extent of it then. The God-honest truth is that you are terrible for all women. Corruption follows you like a stench as you embody all the sordid parts of man.*
> *In no shape or form do you deserve mercy, but my granddaughter certainly did. Every*

day since she's been gone, I have profoundly wished she would have been spared from your grasp, which is why it pains me to write that I'm going to help you. Though, first I must admit why I have made this choice so you can better understand.

As you know, Christie meant a great deal to me, and without her, my will to live has dwindled to nothing. At the beginning I swore it was revenge I yearned for, but I was wrong. I want to move on to a different life, one free of grief. I can only guess that someone like you doesn't believe in heaven, but I do. Therefore, by the grace of God, I'm going to share with you how to free yourself to help my chances at the pearly gates. Brace yourself for the solution, because it is not an easy task.

You will need the human heart of a mother, beating or not, and an open flame to burn it in.

Once you have done this, your troubles will be cured.

Good Luck,
and get the hell
out of my house,
Debra
Peterson.

Debra's letter floored me like a hit from a prized fighter. I couldn't believe what I had just read. Finally, I had proof that it was real; my suspicions were proven accurate. But in spite of my fears being legitimized, no weight had been lifted. Apparently only a human heart and a fire could relieve me.

I didn't care how difficult it seemed on paper. I was going to get my hands on an actual heart if it killed me. My mind raced to hospitals, morgues, and cemeteries—anywhere I could find the precious organ inactive. Waiting for another night didn't even occur to me, I was quickly determined to put an end to the curse that night.

Letter and jacket in hand, I ran out the back and got in my car. Her dried blood caked on my shirt irritated my skin and made me itchy as I Googled local obituaries. Conveniently I found a website with the most recent deaths in Cook County. I glanced at the page still parked on Debra's street, but decided to look more into it elsewhere. Sitting in front of her house whilst covered in her blood with the police potentially on their way made me uneasy (Go figure). Without wasting anymore time I started my car and pulled a U-turn in the quiet residential road.

About a mile away, I passed an unlit police cruiser headed the direction I had fled from.

Former Cook County resident, Kathleene H. Carlin, forty-eight and mother of three, was meant to be my saving grace that night. I chose her mainly because her funeral was just two days before and her burial site was in a remote cemetery outside the city. Since I was in Debra's neck of the woods, I was about twenty-five minutes out. Though with my tense stop at Home Depot for a shovel and pick axe, it was stretched to forty.

My time at the place where doers get more done didn't go by without any curious or concerned looks. Both employees and customers alike easily noticed me. The jacket I retrieved from Debra's covered MOST of the blood, but my appearance was still rough and sickly. I was visibly shivering, still itchy, and mumbling to myself on the way to the gardening section. I knew they were all staring, but I didn't care nor did I return a glance. I was too afraid it might be a woman with her eyes tightly on me.

The Sacred Heart cemetery was ominously quiet as expected, but even more dark than I imagined. I hadn't been wise enough to buy a flashlight, so I relied on my phone. Fortunately, I found Kathleene's grave without a hitch. Similar to any fresh grave, the grass had yet to grow and just a mound of dirt lay in front of the tombstone. I started to dig right away. Any rational thought would have smartened me up and encouraged me to leave, so I resisted thinking at all and dug like hellbent gopher.

But absent thoughts led to another issue.

You see, more than halfway down to Kathleene's grave, a realization struck me... I didn't have a knife to cut out her heart.

Not only that but where was I going to start my fire? Right there in the cemetery? I guess I was. It was never part of my plan to travel with her body. Driving with a corpse in the trunk or a heart in the center console was something a psycho would do. (And I'm anything but psychotic, right?)

Desperate to find a fast solution—or just a sharp knife and hopefully a gas tank with a lighter—I retreated back to my car by the cemeteries' gates. I searched my trunk, backseats, and in between my front seats and recovered a box cutter and a cheap mini torch lighter. They weren't much, but I felt grateful. And to celebrate and intensify my digging, I did a few bumps in the car. Now ready for surgery, I went around my car to shut the back and intended to head back to the grave site.

But when I turned to head that way, a spotlight landed on my chest, and rose to my face, temporarily blinding me.

The light had been pointed from a Cook County Sheriff's car. Within a minute they were pulled up next to me. Fresh out of the grave, my clothes were smothered in dirt, but luckily, I had left the shovel by Kathleene.

"Sir, can I ask you what you think you're doing out here?" he asked sternly.

I suddenly lacked the ability to speak.

"Sir? What are you doing here?"

"I'm the caretaker." I came up with. "I'm out here taking care."

The officer smirked, sucked his teeth and shook his head. "No, you're not."

"Oh yeah?" I challenged nervously, but trying to sound confident. "How would you know?"

The spotlight ceased and he stepped out of the vehicle, revealing his militant build. He also had a buzz cut and Oakley sunglasses resting on his forehead to go with it. Classic cop shit. He filled out his uniform as if he were wearing a small and he had a sleeve of tattoos leading up to his Apple watch. I'm sure you can probably tell, but I already thought he was a dick.

"Well, let's see." He started. "Did you happen to make a call and report that a man was up here digging up graves? Because about twenty minutes ago, the caretaker did. He's got a house outback." He nodded. "That you?"

I swallowed the dry lump in my throat and tried my luck. "…Yes. And good thing you made it ou-"

"Turn around and put your hands on top of the vehicle."

Not trying to get my shit rocked by a tattooed John Wayne, I did as he said, then he frisked me. He pulled out my box cutter and lighter, then put them on the roof of my car. After that, he slapped cuffs on my wrist. Once I was restrained, he flung me around and unzipped my jacket to frisk me further, but the second he saw the huge splotches of blood on my shirt, he didn't touch me again. My next move was walking to the back of the cruiser as he called for backup.

Before reinforcements had even arrived, he found my letter from Debra, my waning bag of drugs, and seen the grave I dug over yonder. The coke bought me a stay in jail, as well as the attempt of crypt robbing, but it was the 'murder' of Debra Peterson that made sure I never saw home again.

XII

The trial. The end.

During my booking they forced me to take off my filthy clothes and issued me the first of many scrubs I'd be wearing. They weren't as itchy, but they were much colder, which made my come down to sobriety that much worse. I shivered like a withdrawing junkie in the cell, and I'm confident everyone at the jail assumed that I was. By appearance, it was a safe bet.

I didn't initially know that I had been charged with Debra's murder. The police kept me in the dark about it for as long as they could. Of course, they had to break it to me sooner or later, but I think they withheld that information on purpose. I mean, they already had me on crypt digging and possession, so it's not like they were desperate for a reason to keep me. My guess is that they didn't tell me simply because they didn't want to hear the quivering maniac in cell three plead his innocence. To them, it was obvious that I had killed her.

The other men who were locked in the cell at Cook County barely acknowledged me, which was a relief and surprise. In my eyes they were all ACTUAL criminals, and they looked the part, but they still didn't glance my way. A few of them even spread out when I entered the cell. It was like they believed whatever I had was contagious or something.

It makes sense though, looking back at it now. I arrived to the jailhouse with beady eyes, dressed in dark blood and dirt and didn't say much of anything. All I did was sit in the corner and rapidly tap my foot while I gazed at the bars. When my head began to clear I quickly became sick, but not yet sleepy. My thoughts were too persistent. I dwelled over Christie, over Jordan, and over my dad, as well as Debra and how she likely set me up to fail. And when an attorney was attached to my case, that became especially evident.

Paul T. Seymour was his name, and while he didn't outright admit that I made him nervous, I knew it to be true. The cuffs had to stay on during our meetings, and when he wasn't visibly frustrated with my account of what happened, sweat rolled off his balding head like a bad liar. His glasses also fogged up every time.

During our first meeting I was just as hesitant as he was, but Paul still managed to get the whole story out of me. I pretty much just told him the same things I've written here for you. I tried not to hold back; I told him about my relationship with Christie, about my condition, and the symbol and letter I found at Debra's house. None of it did me any good though. Not even the part regarding the letter, which he apparently had already seen.

I feel like an idiot for confessing this now, but I wholeheartedly believed that Debra's letter was going to save my ass. In my mind it was solid proof that I didn't kill her, hence why I believed it was destined to expunge the murder charge. The letter she had written clearly implied that she was suicidal, and I thought that was my get-out-of-jail-free card. Surely after reading the letter, no one could think that I actually murdered her. I could deal with a drug charge and the crypt stuff, no problem. Eventually I convinced myself that all I'd receive was a slap on the wrist…

Attorney Paul T. Seymour, however, was quick to tell me that a piece of junk mail wouldn't get me far.

"Junk mail?" I harshly cramped my face. "Who said anything about junk mail? This was a letter, handwritten by Debra, and meant for me. I found it tucked in a jacket I left at her house last Thanksgiving. Have you even read it?"

"Oh, I've read it, all right. However, I'm questioning the fact whether *you* have read it or not. The only piece of paper found in your vehicle was a personal advertisement for Direct TV. The document was folded in your center console and addressed to one, Debra Peterson."

"No! It was a letter written by her and addressed to *me*! It's literally the only reason I was at the cemetery that night."

"Besides to dig up Kathleene, right?"

"Right, but only because the letter told me so."

"Mhm." He hummed, then pulled his brown leather briefcase closer and retrieved a folded piece of paper from inside. Paul then slid it across the table to me. "Is this the letter, Mr. Morgan?"

Carefully I undid the folds and examined the paper. It was the letter, exactly as I had last seen it, but a few more wrinkles added. I confirmed this to Paul, and in response he took it from my hands and snapped it taut twice.

"Brady, this is the Direct TV junk mail I was referring to. There is nothing addressed to you on the entire document, and because I'm on your side, I should tell you what the prosecutor's narrative is… He states that you've recently quit your job at Toyota due to a drug bender that's consumed you, and in frenzied search for funding for your fix, you decided to rob Debra Peterson's. Things didn't pan out like you hoped, and you killed her in panic once she called the authorities."

"But that's a bunch of shit! I wasn't there to rob *or* kill her! I was only there to get help."

"I know, I know. That's what you've told me, but your prints are all over the house. They're even on the weapon used to kill her."

"No, that's impossible. I-I never even touched the knife! She did it to herself! Please, you gotta believe me. You have to get me out of this."

"I'm your attorney, Mr. Morgan, of course I believe you...but the jury? I don't think they'll buy your story."

And he was right. The jury hardly considered my side. Yet they were still sympathetic to my 'illness'. Everyone in the courtroom saw it firsthand, and I think that's part of what sealed my fate.

The room was almost filled solely by women, including the Judge herself. They couldn't take their eyes off me during the proceedings, and whenever I did peak over to them, the women of the jury were either raking the flesh off their arms or tracing bloody designs in their chest. Fortunately, I was able to avoid them for the most part, but the Judge couldn't be ignored as easy.

In spite that the woman was assumingly pushing seventy, honorable Judge Tollefson had the demeanor of an inexpensive hooker. She regularly referred to me by pet names that no one else seemed to hear, winked at me when our eyes rarely met, and puckered her lips to send me kisses across the room. And when none of those received the reaction that she longed for, she took it to ghastly measures.

While tuned out to the hearing, my eyes were safely fixed on Debra's letter. I sat trying to piece it all together, just like I had from the start and still today. Up until this point every single person who had ever read the letter claimed it said the same thing; that Debra's movie watching experience could be amplified by buying the HBO package. One time Paul even tried to point out the company's bright logo printed on the paper, but it just wasn't there for me.

For the life of me, I can't figure out why it was hard to accept that Debra must've hexed the letter as well. Probably just denial, I suppose. By then I was only a little less confused than I was at the beginning. But even now, I can't expect to have all the answers in front of me, and I don't want them anyway. I'm afraid it still wouldn't make any sense. Nothing has so far. Like, why was it so difficult for me to wrap my head around that the old witch who cursed me, had also tricked my eyes into thinking I was reading her writing? I really can't say, but I was in the midst of that thought when Judge Tollefson got a reaction out of me.

Followed by a thunderous, wet thud, there was suddenly a severed wrinkled breast plopped on Debra's letter. My attention fled to the sender before she tossed the other tit my way. Her bloody hand was fishing inside her black robe as she expressed a giddy smile.

I screamed immediately, then stood, retched, puked, and attempted to race out of the courtroom without thinking. The burly bailiff sacked my ass within seconds and escorted me back to holding where I could calm down. So, knowing how that must've looked and what Paul had to work with, I can't really be angry at him for pleading not guilty for reason of insanity. What else was he supposed to do? Just send the maniac to prison with the normal criminals?

Today's the day! My last day of hell, that is (Or maybe it'll be my first day if the Bible is speaking facts). I've told you my story on how I wound up here, and now I have enough closure to move on and do what needs to be done. And it's about time. Things are only getting worse here with the nurses.

Some new hires were introduced to me. All women, and all clearly under Debra's lasting will.

I'm sure you're as sick as everybody else is these days and you want the gritty details on my suicide. It's only natural that you're curious, I get it. But guess what you sick fuck? I'm not going to tell you. I'll only give you a big hint.

Throughout writing this journal, I've thought about Christie and Debra a lot. Before I met her, long before actually, I used to fantasize about being with a woman like Christie. She wasn't just stunning; she had everything you'd want in a girl. Perfect across the board. I used to think that if I ever met a woman like that, I'd dedicate my life to her in a heartbeat.

But then I must've changed.

I fell hard for the excess today's world offers so cheaply. I never knew when it was too much, or when it was time to grow up. Many men have made the same mistakes and many men will continue to make them. And perhaps they deserve the same hand of fate I was dealt. There's nothing like drowning in your own madness to see how sleazy you are. In some ways, it cured me as a man. As previously said, I would have dedicated my life to Christie if I had found her earlier in life, but by the time we met, she was the only one who could dedicate their life.

I aim to change that shortly.

And then that brings me to Grandma Debra, Christie's guardian angel in a way. Why have I been thinking of her? Well, aside from the fact she's a part of some ancient witch tribe or whatever, I've been thinking about her final moments. To be more specific, I think about *how* she went about killing herself. It was pretty barbaric; a knife straight in the throat. It made for quite the mess, but I've found myself admiring it lately. With the lack of choices for myself, I've considered a similar route.

But I don't have a knife.

All I have is the pen I've kept hidden to write this.

Thank you for reading my story,
and be careful who you fall in love with and
how you treat them.

Brady Allen Morgan.

Milton Keynes UK
Ingram Content Group UK Ltd.
UKHW021502301024
450479UK00012B/296

9 798986 717661